The Ogre Downstairs

ALSO BY DIANA WYNNE JONES

Archer's Goon
Aunt Maria
Believing Is Seeing: Seven Stories
Castle in the Air
Dark Lord of Derkholm
Dogsbody
Eight Days of Luke
Fire and Hemlock
Hexwood
Hidden Turnings:
A Collection of Stories Through Time and Space
The Homeward Bounders
Howl's Moving Castle
Power of Three
Stopping for a Spell
A Tale of Time City
The Time of the Ghost
Warlock at the Wheel and Other Stories
Year of the Griffin

The Worlds of Chrestomanci
Book 1: Charmed Life
Book 2: The Lives of Christopher Chant
Book 3: The Magicians of Caprona
Book 4: Witch Week
Mixed Magics (Stories)
The Chronicles of Chrestomanci, Volume I
(Contains books 1 and 2)
The Chronicles of Chrestomanci, Volume II
(Contains books 3 and 4)

The Dalemark Quartet
Book 1: Cart and Cwidder
Book 2: Drowned Ammet
Book 3: The Spellcoats
Book 4: The Crown of Dalemark

Diana Wynne Jones

The OGRE Downstairs

Greenwillow Books

An Imprint of HarperCollins*Publishers*

Library of Congress Cataloging-in-Publication Data
Jones, Diana Wynne.
The ogre downstairs.
Summary: When a disagreeable man with two boys marries a widow with three children, family adjustments are complicated by two magic chemistry sets which cause strange things to happen around the house.
[1. Family life—Fiction. 2. Magic—Fiction] I. Title. PZ7.J6840g 1990 [Fic] 89-11741
ISBN 0-688-09195-4

New Greenwillow Edition, 2002: ISBN 0-06-029883-9

10 9 8 7 6 5 4 3 2 1

For Richard,
who thought of Indigo Rubber,
and Micky,
who helped with the chemicals

The Ogre Downstairs

Chapter 1

aspar came into the hall one afternoon with a bag of books on one shoulder and a bag of football clothes on the other and saw his brother carrying a large square parcel. "What's that?" he said.

"It's the Ogre," Johnny said gloomily. "He's trying to bribe me now."

"Bribe you to do what?" said Caspar.

"Be a sweet little boy, I expect," said Johnny with the utmost disgust. "Let's open it before Malcolm gets in, shall we?"

Caspar, very intrigued, and also quite unreasonably annoyed that Johnny should get a present and not he, led the way to the sitting room door and prepared to sling his bag of books across the room into the red armchair. The bag had almost left his hand, when he saw a large pair of feet sticking out from beyond this chair. Above the chair back was an open newspaper and, below the newspaper, Caspar could just see a section of grizzled black hair. The Ogre himself was in possession. Caspar caught the bag at the top of its swing and retreated on tiptoe.

"He's in there," he mouthed to Johnny.

"Blast!" said Johnny, none too softly. "I thought he was in his study. Let's go upstairs."

They hurried up the stairs, Johnny hugging his parcel, Caspar lugging his two bags. Since Caspar was so laden and Johnny, though smaller, a great deal more hefty and very eager to open his parcel besides, their progress was noisy, and shook the house a little. It was the kind of thing the Ogre could be trusted to notice. His voice roared from beneath.

"Will you boys be *quiet!*"

They sighed. Johnny said something under his breath. They finished climbing on tiptoe, at half-speed. Both knew, by instinct, that it would be unwise to provoke the Ogre further. So far, he had not hit any of them, but they had a feeling that it was only a matter of time before he did, and that it was an experience to be put off as long as possible.

"He's allergic to noise," said Johnny, as they reached their bedroom.

"And boys," Caspar said bitterly.

The Ogre was their stepfather, and he had been married to their mother for a month now. All three children had found it the most miserable month of their lives. They alternated between wishing themselves dead and wishing the Ogre was.

"I don't see why she had to marry him. We were quite all right as we were," Johnny said, as he had said several hundred times before. They halted, according to custom, at the door of their room, for Caspar to hurl his bags one after another onto his bed. Then they set out to wade through comics, books, records, toffee-bars, and sixteen different construction kits, to the one clear piece of floor.

The two boys had disliked the Ogre on sight, despite their mother's glowing description of him. He was large and black-browed and not at all interested in children. He was divorced. His first wife had left him years ago and gone to live abroad—and Caspar's opinion was that he did not blame her, considering what the Ogre and his two sons were like. Their own mother was a widow. Their father had been killed in an air-crash six years before. And, as Johnny kept saying, they had all got on very nicely until the Ogre came along. Of course, they had pretended to their mother—not to hurt her feelings—that they did not think too badly of the Ogre. But, after his second visit—when they were still thinking of him as Mr. McIntyre—their mother had said she was actually going to marry him. Quite appalled, they had escaped to the kitchen as soon as they could, to hold a council of war about him.

"I think he's frightful," Caspar had said frankly. "And I bet he listens to commercial pop. He's bound to, with low eye-brows like that." Since then, alas, they had discovered that the Ogre listened to nothing but news, and required absolute silence while he did so.

"Stepfathers are always frightful," Johnny had agreed, with the air of one who had got through several hundred.

"What do they do?" Gwinny asked nervously.

"Everything. They're perfect Ogres. They eat you as soon as look at you," Johnny had answered. Upon which Gwinny had looked tearful and said she would run away if Mr. McIntyre was an Ogre. And he was. They all knew it now.

As Johnny put down his parcel in the clear patch and pushed aside a bank of other things to make more room, Gwinny came in. "Mummy thought she heard you," she said. "Oh, what's that?"

"A present from the Ogre, for some reason," Johnny said.

"He gave it to me in the hall just now and said it might keep me out of mischief."

Gwinny had been looking offended, and a trifle puzzled. The Ogre could not be said to be friendly with any of them, but, of all three, it was Johnny he liked least. But this explanation relieved her mind. "Oh, *that* kind of present," she said, and even smiled.

Caspar shot a sharp look at her. Gwinny, perhaps from being the youngest and a girl, sometimes showed a regrettable tendency to like the Ogre. It was Gwinny who had first met him, in fact. She had tried to go to the library by herself and had got off the bus at quite the wrong stop. She had wandered for an hour, miserable and lost, with tears trickling down her face, and people passing right and left, taking no notice of her condition whatsoever. Then the Ogre had stopped and asked her what was the matter. And Caspar conceded that Gwinny had a right to be grateful. The Ogre had taken her to the library, then to a cafe for ice cream, and finally brought her home in his car when Caspar and Johnny were out looking for her and only their mother was at home. Caspar often thought that, if only he or Johnny (preferably both) had been at home when the Ogre and Gwinny arrived, the worst would never have happened. But that, as they all knew, had been the sole act of kindness ever performed by the Ogre. Therefore Caspar looked at Gwinny.

"I'm not weakening!" she said indignantly. "I've learned the error of my ways. So there. Oh, look, Caspar!"

Caspar looked, to find that Johnny had taken the paper off the parcel to reveal an enormous chemistry set, which he was contemplating with a mixture of exasperation and grudging pleasure. "I've got one of these already," he said.

"But only half that size and almost used up," Gwinny said consolingly.

"Yes, just think of the smells you can make now," Caspar added kindly. He was not at all interested in chemistry himself. The mere sight of the rows of little tubes and the filter-paper and the spirit-lamp made him want to yawn. And when Johnny lifted out the whole lot in its white plastic container and discovered a second layer of packed tubes and chemicals underneath, it was as much as Caspar could do to show polite interest. "Just like chocolates," he said, and threw himself down on his bed. There, by sweeping aside a pile of books and scattering Johnny's colored crayons, he was able to reach the switch that controlled his record player and turn it on. The LP left ready on the turntable began to revolve. Caspar dropped the needle into the groove and lay back to listen to his favorite group.

Johnny, squatting over the ranks of chemicals, was now grinning happily. "I say, there's everything here," he said. "I can do things we don't even do at school. What do you think this is?" He lifted out a tube labelled *Vol. Pulv.* Gwinny had no idea. Caspar shook his head, and shouted above the mounting wail of a synthesizer and a roll of drums, "I don't know. Shut up for this guitar-solo!"

Johnny continued to lift out tubes and bottles full of substances he had never seen before: *Irid. Col., Animal Spirits, Misc. Pulv., Magn. Pulv., Noct. Vest., Dens Drac.,* and many more. There was a pipette, glass rods, a stand for test-tubes, a china crucible. It really was a magnificent set. He was forced to admit that the Ogre had done him proud— although Gwinny could not hear him admit it, because

Caspar's record had reached its loudest track by then.

At that moment, someone thumped on the door. They all looked at one another. "Wait a minute!" said Caspar. Then he shouted, *"Go away!"* knowing it would be useless.

Sure enough, the door opened and Malcolm, the Ogre's younger son, stood in the entrance looking righteous. By that time, Johnny had whipped the brown paper wrapping across the open chemistry set, and he and Gwinny had moved in front of it.

"My father says you're to turn that damned thing off," reported Malcolm. His eyes wandered disapprovingly round the room as he said it. "At once."

"Oh, he does, bay jewve, does he?" said Caspar. Malcolm's posh accent always set his teeth on edge. "Suppose Ay dewn't?"

"Then you'll catch it, won't you?" Malcolm retorted coolly. He was quite equal to anything Caspar could say or do, although he was a year younger. They suspected that his dreadful pallid coolness came from having been at a posh boarding school until this term. Now, alas, Malcolm went to the same school as Caspar and Johnny.

Unfortunately, as so often, Malcolm's remark was true. Well aware that he *would* catch it, Caspar grudgingly leaned over and turned the sound down, right in the middle of the best song.

"He said off," Malcolm pointed out.

As if to underline his correctness, the Ogre's voice boomed out from downstairs. *"Right off, I said!"*

Caspar obeyed, with black hatred in his heart.

Malcolm, meanwhile, looked coolly to where Johnny and Gwinny were crouching in front of the chemistry set. "What are you sitting on there, Melchior?" he said.

Johnny ground his teeth. "None of your business."

Caspar's rage grew. If anything, he hated Malcolm calling Johnny Melchior even more than Johnny did, because he knew it was a dig at his own absurd name. It was typical of Malcolm to find a convenient way of insulting them both at once. He had called Gwinny Balthazar—only Gwinny had mistaken what he said and had gone to her mother in tears because Malcolm said she was going bald. After that, Malcolm stuck simply to Melchior, and maddening it was, too.

Malcolm ran his eyes once more over the crowded room and turned to leave. "I must say," he said, "I kept this room—"

But he had said this too often before. All three of them joined in. "—much taidier when it was maine."

"Well, I did," said Malcolm. "It's a perfect pigsty now."

Caspar lost his temper and threw himself off his bed and across the room, stumbling and crunching among the things on the floor. *"Get out, you!"* Malcolm prudently dodged out onto the landing, sniggering slightly. The snigger was too much for Caspar. He dived out after Malcolm, roaring insults, and the other two followed hastily to see, as they hoped, justice done.

From below, the Ogre roared once again for silence. No one attended. For, out on the landing, Malcolm was standing defensively above a chemistry set identical to the one the Ogre had given Johnny.

"Look at that!" Gwinny said shrilly.

"If you spoil it," Malcolm said, shriller still, "I'll tell my father."

"As if I wanted to touch it!" said Johnny. "I've got one

the same. So there!"

"So you're not the little favorite you thought you were," added Caspar.

"It isn't fair!" proclaimed Gwinny, voicing Caspar's secret thoughts on the subject too. "Why does he give you two a present and not *us*?"

"Because you're such little frights," said Malcolm. "And Douglas hasn't got anything, either."

"That's because he's a big fright," said Caspar. "Beside Douglas, even your frightfulness pales."

At this, Malcolm put his head down and tried to charge Caspar in the stomach. Caspar dodged. Malcolm ran on into the banister, so that the house shook with the impact. Gwinny and Johnny cheered. The Ogre shouted for quiet. Again no one attended. Caspar saw he now had Malcolm at his mercy and caught his head under one arm. Malcolm yelled and kicked to get free, but Caspar had a whole month of sneers and sniggers to revenge and not even the Ogre would have made him let go just then. Gwinny shouted encouragements. Johnny shrieked advice about where to hit Malcolm next.

The door on the other side of the landing was torn open, and Douglas, like a giant aroused, entered the fray. Douglas was almost as tall as the Ogre, and old enough for his voice to have broken, so that the roar with which he charged down on Caspar was shattering. *"Leave him alone! He's younger than you!"* He tore Caspar and Malcolm apart. The banister reverberated. Caspar protested. Malcolm accused. Johnny and Gwinny yelled at Douglas. Below, the roars of the Ogre became a continuous bull-like bellowing.

"What *is* going on?"

Caspar looked up under Douglas's arm. His mother was standing at the head of the stairs, looking hurt and harassed. Since she had married the Ogre, that hurt and harassed look had scarcely ever left her face. It did not help to make them feel kindly toward the Ogre.

Nobody spoke. Douglas shoved Caspar away and backed to the other side of the landing, beside Malcolm. Caspar backed similarly, between Johnny and Gwinny, and both families stood glowering at one another, breathing heavily.

Sally McIntyre looked from one side to the other, and sighed. "I wish you'd all try to remember there are five of you now," she said. "This was the most awful din."

"Sorry, Sally," said Malcolm and Douglas at once, in a well-behaved chorus.

"And Caspar," said Sally, "Jack says you're welcome to play records any time he's out."

"Big deal!" said Caspar, not at all well-behaved. "What am I supposed to do when he's always in?"

"Do without," said Douglas. "*I* could do without Indigo Rubber, too, for that matter. They stink."

"So does your guitar-playing," Johnny retorted, in Caspar's defense.

"Now, *now*, Johnny," said his mother. "Will you three all come in here a minute, please."

They herded moodily back into the boys' room and looked mournfully at their mother's harrowed face.

"Gracious, what a mess!" was the first thing she said. Then, "Listen, all of you, how many times have I got to tell you to be considerate to poor Malcolm and Douglas? It's very hard on them, because they've had to give up having separate rooms *and* change schools, too. They're having a far more difficult time than you are." There was a heavy-breathing silence, in which Caspar managed not to point out that Malcolm, in particular, made sure that they had a difficult time, too. "It will be better," said Sally, "when we can afford a larger house. Just have patience. And, in the meantime, suppose we tidy this room a little." She stooped to pick up the brown paper at her feet and revealed the chemistry set. "Wherever did you get this?"

"The O—Jack gave it me just now," said Johnny.

Sally's worn face broke into an enchanted smile. "Wasn't that kind of him!" she exclaimed. She picked up the lid of the box and examined it lovingly. They watched her glumly. Quite the worst part of the whole business was the way the Ogre seemed to have cast a spell on their mother, so that whatever he did she thought he was right. "How lavish!" she said. "Nontoxic, guaranteed nonexplosive— Oh, you must be pleased with this, Johnny!"

"He gave one to Malcolm, too," Johnny said.

"That was thoughtful," said Sally. "Then he won't feel left out."

"But *we* do, Mummy," said Gwinny. "He didn't give anything to me and Caspar. Or Douglas," she added, not wishing the Ogre to outdo her in fairness.

"Oh, I do wish you'd be *reasonable,* Guinevere," said Sally unreasonably. "You know we're hard up just now. Come and set the table and stop complaining. And this room is to be tidy before supper. I'll ask Jack to make an inspection."

This threat was enough to cause Johnny and Caspar a little energetic work. By the time the Ogre's heavy feet were heard on the stairs, Caspar had piled books, papers, and records in a sort of heap by the wall, and Johnny had pushed most of the loose construction kits under his bed and the cupboard, so that, apart from the chemistry set, the floor was almost clear.

The Ogre stood in the doorway with his hands in his pockets and his pipe in his mouth and looked round the room with distaste. "You do like to live in squalor, don't you?" he said. "I suppose all those toffee-bars *are* an essential part of your diet? OK, I'll report a clear floor. How are you getting on with that chemistry set?"

"I like it," Johnny said, with a polite smile. "But I've been too busy clearing up to use it yet."

The Ogre's heavy eyebrows went up, and he looked rather pointedly round the room. "I'll leave you to it, then," he said. A thought struck him. "I suppose I ought in fairness to make a surprise inspection over the way," he said. They watched him turn and walk across the landing. They saw him open the door to Malcolm's and Douglas's room. They waited hopefully. It would be wonderful if, for once, it was those two who got into trouble.

Nothing happened, however, except for a surprisingly strong stench, which swept across the landing and made Caspar cough. Malcolm's voice followed it. "This chemistry set is positively brilliant, Father! Look at this."

"Having fun, are you?" said the Ogre, and he shut the door rather hastily and went downstairs.

"Pooh!" said Caspar.

"I just like that!" said Johnny. "If it had been us making a smell like that, we wouldn't half have got it! All right, then. Watch me after supper. I'll make the worst stink you ever smelled, and if he says anything, I'll say, what about Malcolm?"

Johnny was as good as his word. After supper, he set to work in the middle of the carpet, mixing all the strongest and likeliest-looking things from the various tubes and vials and heating them with the spirit-lamp to see what happened. When he found a good smell, he poured it carefully into a tooth-mug and mixed another. The savor of the room went through rotten cabbage, elderly egg, moldy melon, gasworks, and bad breath; blue smoke hung about in it. Caspar, who was lying on his bed doing history homework, coughed considerably, but he bore it in a good cause.

When Gwinny came in instead of going to bed, she was exquisitely disgusted. She sat beside Johnny in her pink nightdress, wriggling her bare toes and pretending to smoke one of the Ogre's pipes that she had stolen. "Eeugh!" she said, and peered at Johnny's flushed face through the gathering smoke. "We look like a witches' convent. Caspar looks like a devil looming through the smoke."

"Coven," said Caspar. "Devil yourself."

Giggling, Gwinny stuck her spiky hair out round her head and carefully tapped some of the ash out of the pipe into the tooth-mug. The mixture fizzed a little. "Do you think it'll explode now?" she asked hopefully.

"Shouldn't think so," said Johnny. "Move, or you'll get burned."

"Is it smelly enough?" asked Gwinny.

"I still haven't found the one Malcolm got," admitted Johnny.

"Try a dead fish or so. That should do it," Caspar suggested.

Gwinny squealed with laughter.

"Gwinny!" boomed the voice of the Ogre. *"Are you in bed?"*

Gwinny dropped the pipe, jumped up and fled. In her hurry, she knocked the tooth-mug flying and Johnny was too late to save it. Half the mixture spilled on the carpet. The rest splashed muddily on Gwinny's legs and nightdress. Gwinny squealed again as she raced for the door. "It's *cold*!" But she dared not stop to apologize. She continued racing, up the next stairs and into her little room on the top floor. She left behind her the most appalling smell. It was worlds worse than the one Malcolm had produced. It was so horrible that it awed them. They were staring at one another in silence, when Gwinny began to scream.

"Caspar! Johnny! Caspar! Oh, come *quickly*!"

Chapter 2

aspar and Johnny pelted up to Gwinny's room regardless of noise. Johnny thought she was on fire, Caspar that she was being eaten away by acids. They burst into the room and stood staring. Gwinny did not seem to be there. Her lamp was lit, her bed empty, her window shut, and her dollhouse and all her other things arranged around as usual, but they could not see Gwinny.

"She's gone," said Caspar helplessly.

"No, I haven't," said Gwinny, her voice quivering rather. "I'm up here." Both their heads turned upward. Gwinny appeared to be hanging from the ceiling. Her shoulders were lodged in the corner where the roof stopped sloping and turned into flat ceiling, her bony legs were dangling straight down beneath her, and her hands were nervously clasped in front of her. She looked a bit like a puppet. "And I can't come down," she added.

"However did you get up?" demanded Johnny.

"I sort of floated," said Gwinny. "I went all light after that stuff splashed on me, and while I was getting into bed I got so light that I just went straight up and stayed here."

"Lordy!" said Johnny. "Suppose the window had been open!" It was a nasty thought. Both boys had visions of a light, leaf-like Gwinny floating out into the night and then up and up, unable to stop, like a hydrogen balloon.

"Let's get her down," said Caspar. "Come on."

By standing on the bed, Caspar thought he could just reach Gwinny's feet, if he jumped as he reached. Johnny stood in front of the bed to help catch her. Caspar got on the bed and jumped. His fingers brushed Gwinny's feet, but he could not get a grip. To his annoyance, the slight push he had given her was enough to send Gwinny bobbing gently out into the middle of the room, quite out of reach.

"Oh dear!" said Gwinny. "Could you lasso me or something?"

Johnny took the cord off Gwinny's dressing-gown to try. But he remembered he had never been able to make a lasso that worked. "I'll throw it," he said. "You catch it. Both hands and carefully, mind." He threw the cord upward—quite a good shot. It hit Gwinny's chest and slithered away down her legs. But Gwinny had always been hopeless at catching things. She missed the cord and went bobbing and twirling away toward the window with the movement.

"That's no good," said Caspar. "She'll be all night before she gets hold of it. Gwinny, can you work yourself along the ceiling, back over the bed, and I'll have another go at catching you."

"I'll try," Gwinny said doubtfully. She put up one hand and pushed at the ceiling. The next moment, to the surprise of all three, she was swooping through the air toward the bed. Caspar raced after her, but, by the time he reached the bed, Gwinny had rebounded from the sloping roof and swooped out into the middle of the ceiling again. "Ooh!" she said, with her spiky head bobbing excitedly against the cord of the light. "That was ever such a nice feeling! I think I'll do it again." And, to Caspar's exasperation, Gwinny began pushing off with a hand here, then there, swooping this way and that and laughing. Johnny started to laugh, too, because Gwinny looked like a gawky pink chicken with her nightdress and long bony legs.

"We must make her stop being so silly," Caspar said. "Gwinny," he said to the soles of Gwinny's swooping feet, "we've got to get you *down*. Don't you understand? Suppose the Ogre finds you like that."

"He wouldn't be able to catch me," Gwinny said gaily, shooting from the window to the space above the door.

"Yes, he would," said Caspar. "Think how tall he is."

"Yes, but, Caspar," said Johnny, "what'll we do if we do get her down? Won't she just shoot up again?"

"We could tie her down," Caspar suggested.

"Oh no, you won't!" Gwinny called. She pushed off from the wall with her feet and floated on her back across the room, to the far corner. And there she lay, with her stomach and toes gently brushing the ceiling and a complacent smile on her face. "Try and catch me now," she said.

They saw it was no use expecting her to be sensible. "Do you think we could get rid of the chemicals somehow, and get her down that way?" Caspar said.

"It might wash off," said Johnny.

"Let's try," said Caspar.

They raced down two floors to the bathroom. There, Johnny seized the big mop that was used to wash the floor and Caspar seized the back-brush, and they hurried upstairs again. As they passed the door of Malcolm's and Douglas's room, they heard Douglas call out something about "herd of blinking elephants," but they were too fussed to bother.

Gwinny was lying on her back near the middle of the ceiling now. Johnny raised the dripping mop and aimed it for the part of Gwinny's legs where he thought the chemicals had splashed. But it was not easy to aim a long, top-heavy mop. He hit Gwinny plumb on the backside. She shrieked, "Stop it! It's cold!" and went floundering and scrambling and bobbing out of reach, like an upside-down pink crab, with a muddy splodge on the back of her nightdress. Caspar got onto the bed and clawed at her legs with the back-brush as soon as they came near.

"Stop it, you beast!" said Gwinny, and scrambled back across the ceiling.

Caspar jumped onto a chair on the other side of the room and tried to reach her from there. Johnny lofted the mop and prodded at her as she passed. Gwinny squealed with silly laughter and scrambled out of reach again. They pursued her. Caspar went leaping from chair to bed and back again. Johnny charged this way and that, prodding, and Gwinny scuttled and squealed all over the ceiling. Then Johnny, not looking where he was going, kicked the dollhouse over with a crash, scattering little tables and chairs and dollhouse people all over the room.

Gwinny turned over and drummed her heels on the ceiling, pointing furiously. "How dare you! Look what you've done! Pick them all up!"

"You come and do it," said Johnny cunningly.

"I can't, I can't, I can't!" said Gwinny, drumming away for all she was worth.

There were footsteps, and the shattering voice of Douglas bawled from the stairs, "Stop that din, can't you! Some of us are trying to do homework."

Gwinny's heels stopped. Caspar and Johnny exchanged alarmed looks. Without a word, they got down and began collecting the chairs, tables, and dolls. But the damage was done. Behind the feet of Douglas retreating, they heard a much more distant door slam. They waited. Heavy footsteps started upstairs. They galvanized Caspar. He leaped up, seized the mop, and pointed it at Gwinny.

"Quick! Catch hold of that, Gwinny, and don't let go."

Gwinny was only too ready to do as he told her. She hung on to the wet end while Caspar heaved on the stick. It was extraordinarily hard work. Gwinny seemed a good deal heavier upwards, as it were, than she ever was on the ground. Johnny flung the last table into the dollhouse and helped Caspar heave. Slowly Gwinny was dragged down. Slowly and remorselessly the Ogre's feet climbed the stairs. Once she was within reach, Gwinny was so terrified of rising again that she seized Johnny's hair to hold herself down with.

"What do we do now?" said Johnny, through a grin of agony.

"Bed. The covers might hold her down," gasped Caspar.

They towed the floating Gwinny over to her bed and attempted to put her into it. Gwinny did her best to help, but nothing seemed to stop her floating away upward every time they tried to put her legs between the sheets.

The Ogre's feet crossed the landing and began on the last flight.

Gwinny flung her arms round Johnny in terror. While she was anchored that much, Caspar let go, picked up all the bed-covers, flung them over her floating legs and flung himself after them. As the Ogre's feet came up the last stairs, Johnny jumped onto Gwinny too and sat on her stomach.

When the Ogre tore open the door and stood glowering, he saw Gwinny in bed, Caspar sitting on one end of it, Johnny in the middle, and all their faces turned to him in not-quite-innocent alarm. The only thing out of place was the wet mop Gwinny seemed to be nursing and a muddy splotch on the pillow.

"What the dickens are you all doing here?" said the Ogre.

"Telling her a bedtime story," said Caspar breathlessly.

"Why does it need two of you and all this din?" demanded the Ogre.

Caspar and Johnny could not think. Gwinny said brightly, "They were doing it with funny voices to make me laugh."

"Were they?" said the Ogre. "Well, they can just *stop*!"

"Oh no," said Johnny. "We were just near the end. Can't we just finish?"

"No, you just can't," said the Ogre. "Your mother and I are entitled to some peace."

"Please!" they chorused desperately.

"Oh, very well," said the Ogre irritably. "Five minutes. And if I hear another sound there'll be trouble. What are you doing with that filthy mop?"

Again neither Caspar nor Johnny could think. "It's a broomstick," said Gwinny. "The story's about a witch."

"Then you can either do without or change the story," said the Ogre. "I'm taking that back where it came from." He strode over to the bed and tried to wrench the mop out of Gwinny's hands. Gwinny lost her presence of mind and hung on to the mop with all her strength. The force with which the Ogre tore it free raised her a full foot off the bed and Johnny with her. Luckily, Johnny's weight and Caspar's were enough to bring her down again fairly quickly, and the Ogre did not notice their sudden elevation because his foot chanced, at that moment, to kick against the back-brush. He picked it up and looked at it meditatively. "I can think of a very good use for this," he said. "Don't tempt me too far." Then he went away, taking the mop and the brush with him.

They listened tensely to his retreating footsteps. When he had reached the bathroom, Caspar said, "Now what shall we do? We can't sit here all night."

"But I'll be cold on the ceiling," Gwinny whimpered.

"You could take a blanket up with you," Caspar suggested.

"If you could hold her down," said Johnny, "I think I can fix her."

"All right," said Caspar. "But don't be too long."

So Johnny departed downstairs with heavy-footed stealth and Caspar tried to keep Gwinny in place. He found it next to impossible on his own. In a matter of seconds, she was floating clear of the bed, bedclothes and all. "Oh, what shall we do?" she wailed.

"Shut up, for a start," said Caspar.

The bedclothes slid away and Caspar was hanging on to Gwinny's nightdress. There was a slow tearing sound. Gwinny whimpered and began to rise again, gently but surely. Caspar was forced to let go of her nightdress and catch hold of her ankles. There he hung on desperately. He found, in the end, that if he leaned back, with his head nearly touching the floor and all his weight swinging on Gwinny, he could keep her floating upright about three feet from the floor. They had reached this point when Johnny came swiftly upstairs and entered the room with a bucket of water, looking very businesslike.

"Oh, good," he said, when he saw the position Gwinny was in, and he threw the water over the pair of them.

He had not thought to bring warm water. Gwinny squealed. Caspar gasped and nearly let go. He was about to say some very unkind things to Johnny, when he realized that Gwinny was now much easier to hold down.

"It's working," he said. "Go and get some more."

Johnny turned, beaming with relief, and went galloping away downstairs, bucket clattering. Somewhat to Caspar's annoyance, he did not stop at the bathroom, but went on galloping, right downstairs to the kitchen, because the water ran more quickly from the taps downstairs. Caspar shook his soaking hair out of his eyes and hung on grimly. Gwinny's teeth chattered.

"I'm freezing," she complained. "My nightie's soaking."

"I know," said Caspar. "It's dripping all over me, and I'm sitting in a puddle, if that's any comfort."

After what seemed half an hour, they heard Johnny pounding upstairs again. Caspar was too relieved to worry about the noise he was making. He just listened to Johnny pounding closer and closer and prayed for him to hurry. As Johnny's feet crossed the landing below, a confused noise broke out on the same level. Johnny had started on the last flight of stairs, when Douglas erupted into another shattering roar.

"What the blazes are you doing? There's water pouring through our ceiling!"

Johnny did not answer. They heard his feet climbing faster. Then came the feet of Douglas, pounding behind. Behind that again were other feet. Caspar and Gwinny could only wait helplessly, until the door at last crashed open and Johnny staggered in, red-faced and almost too breathless to move, with water slopping over his shoes out of the bucket.

"Throw it," Caspar said urgently.

Johnny croaked for breath, heaved up the bucket and poured the water over Gwinny, drenching Caspar again in the process. It did the trick. Gwinny dropped like a stone and landed on Caspar. There was a short time when Caspar could not see much and was almost as breathless as Johnny. When he recovered sufficiently to sit up, Douglas was standing behind Johnny, looking as if he had frozen in the middle of shouting something, and behind him were the Ogre and their mother.

"Johnny!" said Sally. "Whatever possessed you?"

"Take him downstairs, Douglas," said the Ogre, "and make him clear it up. These two can clear up here."

"Come on," Douglas said coldly. Johnny departed without a word. There really was nothing to say.

An hour later, when Gwinny had been put to bed in a clean nightdress and everywhere wet mopped dry, Caspar and Johnny went rather timidly into their room, expecting to see the carpet, where the rest of the chemicals had gone, floating against the ceiling—or at least ballooning up in the middle. But the only sign of the spill was a large purple stain and a considerable remnant of bad smell. Much relieved, Caspar opened the window.

"It must only work on people," Johnny said thoughtfully.

"We'd better clear it up," said Caspar.

Johnny sighed, but he obediently trudged off to the bathroom for soap and water. He returned still thoughtful and remained so all the time he was rubbing the carpet with the Ogre's towel. The stain came off fairly easily and dyed the towel deep mauve.

"Couldn't you have used yours or mine?" said Caspar.

"I did. Douglas made me use them on their room," said Johnny. "Listen. Gwinny got an awful lot of that stuff on her, didn't she? Suppose you use less, so you weren't quite so light, wouldn't you be like flying?"

"Hey!" said Caspar, sitting up in bed. Since he had had to change all his clothes, it had seemed the simplest place to be. "That's an idea! What did you put in it?"

"I can't remember," said Johnny. "But I'm darned well going to find out."

Chapter 3

In the days that followed, Johnny experimented. He made black mixtures, green mixtures, and red ones. He made little smells, big smells, and smells grandiose and appalling. These met the smells coming from Malcolm's efforts and mingled with them, until Sally said that their landing seemed like an affliction to her. But whatever smell or color Johnny made, he was no nearer finding the right mixture. He went on doggedly. He remembered that Gwinny had put pipe-ash in the mixture, so he always made that one of the ingredients.

"Who is it keeps taking my pipes?" demanded the Ogre, and received no answer. And in spite of Johnny's running this constant risk, his efforts were not rewarded. Nevertheless, he persevered. It was his nature to be dogged, and Caspar and Gwinny were thankful for it; for, as Gwinny said, the idea of being really able to fly made it easier to bear the awfulness of everything else.

Each day seemed to bring fresh trials. First there was the trouble over the purple towel, and then the affair of the muddy sweater on the roof, mysteriously found wrapped round the chimney. The Ogre, as a matter of course, blamed Caspar, and, when Caspar protested his innocence, he blamed Johnny. And twice Caspar forgot that the Ogre was at home and played Indigo Rubber—the third time, the noise came from Douglas, but Douglas said nothing and let Caspar take the blame. Then the weather turned cold. The house had very old central heating, which seemed too weak to heat all four floors properly. The bathroom, and the bedroom shared by Sally and the Ogre, were warm enough, but upward from there it grew steadily colder. Gwinny's room got so cold that she took to sneaking down to her mother's room and curling up on the big soft bed to read. Unfortunately, she left a toffee-bar on the Ogre's pillow one evening, and the boys were blamed again. It took all Gwinny's courage to own up, and the Ogre was in no way impressed by her heroism. However, he did find her an old electric heater, which he installed in her room with instructions not to waste electricity.

"*We* don't need to be pampered," Malcolm said odiously. "You should see what it's like at a boarding school before you complain here."

"Quait," said Caspar. "Full of frosty little snobs like you. Why don't you go back there where you belong?"

"I wish I could," Malcolm retorted, with real feeling. "Anything would be better than having to share this pigsty with you."

Nearly a week passed. One afternoon, Caspar was as usual hurrying home in order not to have to walk back with Malcolm, when he discovered himself to be in a silly kind of mood. He knew he was going to have to act up somehow. He decided to do it in the Ogre's study, if possible, because it was the warmest room in the house and also possessed a nice, glossy parquet floor, ideal for sliding on. As soon as he got home, he hurried to the study and cautiously opened its door.

The Ogre was not there, but Johnny was. He was rather gloomily turning ash out of the Ogre's pipes into a tin for further experiments.

"How's it going?" Caspar asked, slinging his bag into the Ogre's chair and sitting on the Ogre's desk to take his shoes off.

Johnny jumped. The Ogre's inkwell fell over, and Johnny watched the ink spreading with even deeper gloom. "He'll know it's me," he said. "He always thinks it's me, anyway."

"Unless he thinks it's me," said Caspar, casting his shoes to the floor. "Wipe it up, you fool. But is the Great Caspar daunted by the Ogre? Yes, he is rather. And the ink is running off the desk into his shoes."

Johnny, knowing he would get no sense out of Caspar in this mood, picked up the Ogre's blotting-paper and put it in the pool of ink. The blotting-paper at once became bright blue and sodden, but there seemed just as much ink as before.

Gwinny came in, hearing their voices. "There's ink running off onto the floor," she said.

"Tell me something I don't know," said Johnny, wondering how one small inkwell always contained such floods of ink.

"I'll do the floor," said Gwinny. "Can't you help, Caspar?"

"No," said Caspar, gliding smoothly in his socks across the floor. He did not see why he should be deprived of his pleasure because of Johnny's clumsiness.

"Well, we think you're mean," said Gwinny, fetching a newspaper from the rack and laying it under the streams of ink.

"The Great Caspar," said Caspar, "is extremely generous."

"Take no notice," said Johnny. "And pass me a newspaper."

Caspar continued to slide. "The Great Caspar," he said kindly, "will slide for your entertainment while you work, lady and gentleman. He has slid before all the crowned heads of Europe, and will now perform, solely for your benefit, the famous hexagonal turn. Not only has it taken him years to perfect, but—"

"Oh, shut up!" said Johnny, desperately wiping.

"—it is also very hazardous," said Caspar. "Behold, the hazardous hexagon!" Upon this, Caspar spun himself round and attempted to jump while he did it. While he was in the air, he saw the Ogre in the doorway, lost his balance, and ended sitting in a pool of ink. From this position, he looked up into the dour face of the Ogre. His own face was vivid red, and he hoped most earnestly that the Ogre had not heard his boastful fooling.

The Ogre had heard. "The Great Caspar," the Ogre said, "appears to have some difficulty with the hexagonal turn. *Get up!* AND GET OUT!"

To complete Caspar's humiliation, Malcolm appeared in the doorway, snorting with laughter. "What *is* a hexagonal turn?" he said.

The Ogre's roar had fetched Sally, too. "Oh, just look at this mess!" she cried. "Those trousers are ruined, Caspar. Don't any of you have the slightest consideration? Ink all over poor Jack's study!"

It was the last straw, being blamed for falling in the ink. Caspar, with difficulty, climbed to his feet. "Poor Jack!" he said, with his voice shaking with rage, and fear at his own daring. "It's always poor, flipping Jack! What about poor *us* for a change?"

The hurt, harrowed look on Sally's face deepened. The Ogre's face became savage, and he moved toward Caspar with haste and purpose. Caspar did not wait to discover what the purpose was. With all the speed his slippery socks would allow, he dodged the Ogre, dived between Malcolm and Sally, and fled upstairs.

There he changed into jeans, muttering. His face was red, his eyes stung with misery, and he could not stop himself making shamed, angry noises. "I wish I was *dead*!" he said, and surged toward the window, wondering whether he dared throw himself out. His progress scattered construction kits and hurled paper about. He knocked against a corner of the chemistry box. It shunted into its lid, which Johnny had left lying beside it, and a tube of some white chemical lying on the lid rolled across it and spilled a little white powder on Caspar's sock as he passed.

Caspar found himself reaching the window in two graceful, slow-motion bounds, rather like a ballet dancer's, except that his socks barely met the floor as he passed. And when he was by the window, instead of stopping in the usual way, his feet again left the floor in a long, slow, drifting bounce. Hardly had he realized what was happening, than he was down again, quite in the usual way, with a heavy bump, on top of what felt like a drawing-pin.

He was so excited that he hardly noticed it. He simply pulled off his sock, and the drawing-pin with it, and waded back with one bare foot to the chemistry set. The little tube of chemical was trembling on the edge of the lid, and white powder was filtering down from it onto the carpet. Caspar's hands shook rather as he picked it up. He planted its stopper firmly in, and then turned it over to read the label. It read *Vol. Pulv.,* which left Caspar none the wiser. But the really annoying thing was that the little tube was barely half full. Either most of it had gone the night Gwinny took to the ceiling, or Johnny had unwittingly used it up since in other mixtures that destroyed its potency. Wondering just how potent the powder was, Caspar carefully put his bare foot on the place where the tube had spilled. When nothing happened, he trod harder and screwed his foot around.

He was rewarded with a delicious feeling of lightness. A moment later, his feet left the ground, and he was hanging in the air about eighteen inches above the littered floor. He was not very light. He gave a scrambling sort of jump to see if he could go any higher, and all that happened was that he bounced sluggishly over toward the window. It was such a splendid feeling that he bounced himself again and went jogging slowly toward Johnny's bed.

"Yippee!" he said, and began to laugh.

He invented a kind of dance then, by jumping with both feet together first to one side and then to the other. Bounce and . . . Bounce and . . . His head swung, his hair flew, and he brandished the tube in his hand. Bounce and . . . Bounce and . . . "Yippee!"

Johnny and Gwinny came soberly and mournfully into the room while he was doing it. For a moment they could not believe their eyes. Then Johnny hastily slammed the door shut.

"I've found it!" said Caspar, bouncing away and waving the tube at them. "I've found it! It's called *Vol. Pulv.* and it works by itself. Yippee!" He suddenly felt himself becoming heavy again and was just in time to bounce himself over to his bed before the powder stopped working and he came down with a flop that made the bedsprings jangle. He sat there laughing and waving the tube at the others.

"How marvelous!" said Gwinny. "You are clever, Caspar."

Johnny came slowly over to the bed. He took the tube and looked at it. "I was going to try this one today," he said.

Caspar looked up at his gloomy face and understood that Johnny, not unreasonably, was feeling how unfair it was that Caspar should discover the secret, when Johnny had worked so hard over it and had just been in dire trouble about the ink as well. "You still need to do a lot of work on it," Caspar said tactfully. "I used it dry, and it ought to be mixed with water. You'll have to work out the right proportions."

Johnny's face brightened. "Yes," he said. "*And* experiment to find out how much you need, not to go soaring right out of the atmosphere. I'll have to do tests on myself, bit by bit."

"That's right," agreed Caspar. "But for goodness sake don't use too much while you do it. The tube's less than half full already."

"I've got eyes," Johnny said crossly. Then, feeling he was being rather ungracious, he added, "I'm the Great Scientist. I think of everything."

He tried to make good this boast by fencing off a corner of the room, so that no accident should happen while the experiments were in progress. For the rest of the evening he sat in his pen, carefully putting the powder, grain by grain, into a test-tube of water, and then bathing his big toe with the result.

"What's the matter with Johnny?" their mother wanted to know, when she came in around bedtime.

Johnny, by this time, was bobbing an inch or so from the floor. He took hold of a chair that was part of his fence to hold himself down, and pretended not to have heard.

"I knocked over one of his experiments this afternoon," Caspar explained anxiously, "and he doesn't want anybody to do it again. Be careful of him. He's very angry."

Sally gave Johnny a puzzled look. "All right, darling. I won't interfere. It was you I wanted to talk to anyway, Caspar."

"About what I said about Jack? I'm sorry," Caspar said hurriedly, dreading a scene. Scenes with his mother were always painful, not because she scolded, but because she believed in absolute honesty.

Sure enough, she said, "That's not quite the point, darling. I could see you were hurt and miserable, and it upset me. Can't you bring yourself to like Jack a little better? He really is very nice, you know."

"Why should I? He doesn't like us," Caspar retorted with equal honesty.

"He tries," Sally said earnestly. "I can think of at least a hundred occasions when he's been very forebearing indeed."

"There are about a thousand when he hasn't," Caspar said bitterly.

"That's partly because you've been so awful," Sally said frankly. "Truly, I'm ashamed of you most of the time—all of you, but particularly you as the eldest."

Caspar's face was red and he wanted to mutter again. He looked over at Johnny. Johnny looked sulkily at his big toe and gave it a slight waggle. He was hating the scene as much as Caspar, and he was also mortally afraid that he was going to rise from his pen any minute and float about. Caspar did his best to send Sally away. "I'm sorry," he said, sounding so sincere and nice that he made himself feel ill. "I will try." He was quite unable to keep up this level of piety. He found himself adding, "I do try, only he keeps blaming me so."

"You must remember," said Sally, "that he isn't really used to children. Malcolm and Douglas have been away at school most of the time, and he simply had no idea what it could be like."

"He's finding out, isn't he?" said Caspar.

Sally laughed. "You can say that again! All right. Good night, darlings. And do try a bit harder in the future."

She went out and shut the door. Johnny gave a sigh of relief, let go of the chair, and bobbed clear of the floor again.

Before he went to bed, he had risen to three feet. Caspar was rather glad to find that there was no horrible smell this time, as the mixture in the test-tube grew stronger. It must have been due to all the other things Johnny had put in. They were discussing it when Malcolm, in his usual manner, knocked and came in despite being told to go away. Johnny was only just in time to pull himself over to the cupboard and pretend to be sitting on top of it.

"My father says you're to put your light out," Malcolm said. His eyes wandered critically to Johnny. "What are you sitting up there with one shoe off for?"

"We've both got one shoe off," said Caspar, stretching out his bare foot and wriggling the toes at Malcolm's face. "It's the badge of our secret society. Now go away."

"You don't think I come in here for pleasure, do you?" Malcolm said, and went away.

Johnny looked anxiously at Caspar. "Do you think he suspected anything?"

"He's far too flipping dim for that," said Caspar. "But you'd better be careful. If he did find out, he'd tell the Ogre like a shot."

"I think I'll stop now," said Johnny. "For tonight." So Caspar washed his big toe for him, and Johnny climbed off the cupboard and went to bed.

The next day, Johnny skipped games and pelted home from school to continue his experiments. When Caspar came in, he found Johnny, again with one shoe off, triumphantly floating just below the ceiling.

"Look at this!" he said. "I could go higher if I put more on, only all the powder's in the water now and I don't want to waste it. Can you take the test-tube and prop it carefully on that stand down there?"

Caspar stood on the cupboard and took the test-tube from Johnny's reaching hand. Then he climbed down and propped it upright in Johnny's pen, while Johnny looked on tensely from the ceiling.

"What are you going to do now?" Caspar asked. "Come down?"

"I think I ought to practice a bit," said Johnny. "You hold the door in case Malcolm comes in."

Caspar stood against the door and watched a little wistfully while Johnny pushed off from the ceiling and swooped this way and that across the room, as Gwinny had done. It looked like enormous fun. Johnny was laughing. And now that he knew what a splendid feeling it was to be nearly as light as air, Caspar could hardly wait to get up there and swoop about himself.

"Hadn't I better shut the window?" he called up at Johnny's whisking feet.

"It's all right," Johnny said happily. "It's quite easy to control where you go. Like swimming, only not such hard work. Watch."

Caspar watched him doing a slow, swooping breaststroke through the air, and yearned to see what a fast overarm would do. "When shall we all try?"

Johnny turned over and trod water, or rather air. "What about going out tonight, after dark, for a fly round town?"

Caspar was about to say that this was the best idea Johnny had had in his life, when there was a thump on the door behind him. He flung himself against it, with his feet braced. "Go away. We're busy."

"Buzz off!" Johnny shouted down from the ceiling.

The doorknob began turning. Caspar grabbed it and held it hard. In spite of this, the knob continued to turn and the door moved slightly. Caspar had not thought Malcolm was so strong. "Go away!" he said.

"I only want to borrow Indigo Rubber," said a much deeper voice than Malcolm's. "What's so special that I can't come in?"

Caspar looked up helplessly at Johnny's alarmed face. "I thought you didn't like Indigo Rubber," he shouted through the door.

"I've come round to them," Douglas called back. "And I've got some friends coming tonight who want to hear it."

"You can't have it," called Caspar.

"But I promised them," said Douglas. "Be a sport."

"You'd no business to promise them my records!" Caspar said, with real indignation. "You can't have them. Go away."

"I knew you'd go and be mean about it," said Douglas. "It's typical. I only want to borrow their second LP for an hour this evening. I won't hurt it, and you can come and listen, if you like. Father's said we can have it in the dining room."

"You should have asked me first," said Caspar. But put like that, Douglas's request was reasonable, and he did not want to be thought mean.

"Tell him to come back for it in five minutes," Johnny whispered from the ceiling. "Then get me some water."

Caspar drew his breath to shout, but Douglas had lost patience. "You are a mean little squit, aren't you?" he said. "It's no good trying to be polite to you. You lend me that record, or watch out!" The doorknob turned sharply under Caspar's hands, and the door began to open.

"Come back in five minutes!" Caspar said desperately, his braced feet sliding.

"And give you time to hide it?" said Douglas. "What kind of a fool do you think I am?" The door opened nearly a foot, and Douglas's leg and shoulder came through the gap. It was clear that the rest of him was following.

Johnny did the only thing he could think of. With a strong thrust at the ceiling and a desperate kick of his legs, he got himself to the open window and, as the door crashed open and Douglas plunged into the room, he pushed himself out of it. And, whether it was the draft from the door, or the different conditions outside, Johnny promptly soared. The last Caspar saw of him was his bare foot and his shoe vanishing upward, beyond the top of the window.

Luckily, Douglas was looking malevolently at Caspar. "Got any more mean excuses?" he said.

"It's not mean. You shouldn't promise things that aren't yours," said Caspar. But his heart was not in the argument. All he could think of was Johnny soaring away into the heavens.

"Well, I'd have asked you this morning, only you'd gone by the time I'd persuaded Father to let me have the dining room," Douglas said. "Are you going to lend it to me, or not?"

"You can have them all. They're down there by my bed. And I've got their new one, too," Caspar said hastily.

"Their new one!" Douglas said delightedly. "Really? 'Brainpan,' you mean?" He waded over to Caspar's bed and went on his knees by the window to sort out the records. Instead of taking the records at once, he knelt there looking disgusted. "I wonder you can hear these," he said. "They're coated with dust. Hasn't anyone ever told you to keep LP's clean? You're ruining them and your stylus."

"I know, but I've lost my cleaner," said Caspar, almost beside himself with impatience to get to the window and see what had become of Johnny.

"I'm not surprised," said Douglas, looking round the crowded room. "You can borrow mine, if you're careful with it. I've got one of those attachments now. Thanks, anyway. I'd better go and give these a clean." And to Caspar's relief, Douglas got up and waded to the door.

Caspar sped to the window and craned out of it. Johnny was not far off. He was clinging like a monkey to the corner of the house, about four feet above the window. "You can come back now," Caspar told him. "He's gone."

"I can't!" Johnny said tensely.

"Why not?"

"It's worn off. I'm stuck. I can't hold on much longer, either."

Caspar felt rather sick. He looked down and realized that the ground was a very long distance away. Worse still, the Ogre's car was now parked on the gravel at the side of the garden. For two very good reasons, Johnny had better not go down. He looked up. The roof and the gutter, which came lower at the back of the house, were only three feet or so above Johnny's head.

"Can you climb up and grab the roof?" he said.

"What do you think I've been *trying* to do?" snapped Johnny. "It's all I can do to stay in one place."

"Then hang on. I'll go out of the trapdoor in the loft," said Caspar, "and see if I can pull you up. Hold on."

"What do you expect me to do? Let go?" said Johnny.

Caspar sped to the door and up the stairs that led to Gwinny's room. The loft was behind a low door opposite Gwinny's. Gwinny came out to see what was going on as Caspar was frenziedly rattling at it.

"You don't pull, you push," she said. "Is something the matter?"

"Yes," said Caspar. "Johnny's stranded halfway up the house and I've got to pull him up from here. Where's the Ogre?"

"In the study, I think. I'll fetch my dressing-gown cord," said Gwinny.

Caspar crashed the door open inward and hurried forward into the loft. There was no proper floor, and he had to jump from joist to joist, which was not easy in the dim light. He was struggling to open the trapdoor to the roof, when Gwinny came crawling after him with the dressing-gown cord in her mouth so that she could use both hands for crawling.

"Th'Ogre," she said indistinctly.

"Where?"

"I don't know," Gwinny said, removing the cord. "But I could hear him shouting at someone. He sounded awfully angry."

"I hope it's Malcolm. And I hope it keeps them both busy," said Caspar. "Help me with this bolt."

It was no easy matter to open the trap. The bolts were rusty, and the Ogre had packed putty round the door itself to keep the rain out after he had fetched the muddy sweater in off the chimney. To Caspar's frantic imagination, it took them an hour to unpack it again. Rust, dust, putty, and cobwebs spattered down on them, and Caspar, unwisely bracing his foot between two joists, managed to put his knee through the plaster floor. But they got the door open in the end. Caspar hastily raised it and stood up into a cold sunset to lower it onto the tiles of the roof. Gwinny stood up beside him.

"Shall I climb out? I'm the lightest," she said.

"No. You're to stay there," said Caspar. "It's dangerous."

He had one leg out over the edge of the trap, when, to his amazement, Johnny, looking white and shaken, appeared over the edge of the roof and started to crawl up it toward him.

"How did you climb up?" said Caspar. Johnny, for some reason, fiercely shook his head at him. "You *must* have done," said Caspar. "You—"

The head and shoulders of the Ogre appeared behind Johnny. Even for the Ogre, they looked grim. All Caspar could do was to make haste to get himself back inside the loft again.

Chapter 4

It seemed that one of the neighbors had seen Johnny clinging to the side of the house and telephoned the Ogre. Probably it was just as well. Johnny had been precious near letting go by the time the Ogre had tied two ladders together and climbed up them. But in every other way it was unfortunate.

The Ogre made the obvious assumption that they had been playing on the roof and that Johnny had slipped off. He sent Johnny to bed without supper. Then he nailed up first the trapdoor, then the loft door, and forbade them all three, on pain of death, to touch either. Douglas, who was ordered in to help with the nailing, and who might have provided Caspar at least with an alibi, said nothing at all, to Caspar's bitter annoyance. He just listened to Caspar being blamed for leading Johnny and Gwinny into danger. And Malcolm—who was supposed to be opening the trapdoor to let the Ogre and Johnny through—arrived in time to listen, too. And he laughed. This so infuriated Gwinny that she bit Malcolm. It was all she could think of on the spur of the moment. So she was in trouble as well. The Ogre called her a vicious little cat and sent her to bed without supper, too.

Caspar supposed he was lucky to be allowed supper himself.

But it was not a comfortable meal. The Ogre had gone downstairs and expressed himself forcibly to Sally after nailing up the
loft, and Caspar could see his mother had been crying. He felt
truly wretched. Douglas and Malcolm were, as usual, well
mannered, sober, and almost totally silent. Caspar sat quite as
silent, wishing the Ogre would not make such a horrible noise
eating. Finally, Sally tried to make conversation by asking
Douglas when his friends were coming.

Douglas replied, quietly and politely, "About eight o'clock,
if that's all right."

"Of course," Sally said cordially. "I'm so glad you've
managed to make some friends already."

"Thank you," Douglas said politely.

"Because it is difficult, when you move to a new school,
isn't it?" Sally said.

"It's not so bad," said Douglas. "Thank you."

Sally gave up. Nobody said anything else. Caspar missed
Gwinny and Johnny acutely, because, if they did nothing else,
they could be counted on to talk.

At the end of supper, Douglas and Malcolm politely
offered to wash up, and Douglas surprised Caspar by turning
to him and asking, equally politely, if he wanted to come to
the dining room and listen to records, too.

"Oh no, thank you," Caspar said hastily. He had had about
enough of Douglas by then.

"That's rather a blessing," Sally said to him in the kitchen,
a little later, "because I want you to go on a secret mission and
take some supper up to Johnny and Gwinny. I know Jack said
they were to go without, but I can't bear to think of them
going hungry. But you must do it with the utmost stealth."

"All right," said Caspar, and looked meaningly at Malcolm, who was still busily and correctly wiping plates. When Sally did not seem to see what he meant, he tried to make her understand by waggling his eyebrows at her.

"Do stop making faces," said Sally. "Malcolm won't tell, will you, Malcolm?"

"Of course not," Malcolm said coldly.

Caspar did not believe him for a moment, but he nevertheless crept upstairs with loaded trays. His task was made easier by the fact that Gwinny had sneaked down to join Johnny. They were both sitting in Johnny's bed sharing a toffee-bar, looking rosy and excited.

"When are we going flying?" Johnny asked.

Caspar had imagined that, after being stranded on the side of the house, Johnny would have had enough of flying, and he was rather taken aback. "When were you thinking of?" he said.

"Not too late," said Johnny.

"I want to look down on all the lights in Market Street," explained Gwinny. "The Christmas lights are up already, did you know?"

"And see the nightlife," said Johnny. "If we're lucky, we might see some vice going on. I've never seen any."

"We've been thinking it out," said Gwinny. "It's awfully cold out, so we'll have to go in coats, with shoes on, and wear gloves."

"And put the flying-mixture on our legs," said Johnny, "under our trousers. Rub on a really good handful, because we don't want it wearing off in the middle of town."

"All right," Caspar said weakly. "About half past ten?"

"And put pillows in our beds," Johnny called after him

as he waded to the door.

Caspar went downstairs again to report his mission accomplished. He was so excited at the thought of going flying that very night that he forgot to refuse when Sally said, "And don't go away upstairs again, Caspar. Come and join us in the sitting room for a change."

"If you like," Caspar said, without thinking, and then realized that he had condemned himself to a whole evening with the Ogre.

Douglas's friends were arriving when he and Sally reached the hall. Caspar took one look at them and was heartily glad that he had refused Douglas's invitation at least. They were all as tall as Douglas and, since none of them were in school clothes, they appeared even more grown up than they were. They carried bundles of records. Two of them had guitars. And they laughed and made jokes that Caspar could not understand. Douglas, as he showed them in, laughed too and made the same sort of jokes in reply. Caspar stared rather, because he had hardly ever seen Douglas laugh before, and because Douglas had changed his clothes and looked just as grown up as his friends.

"Coffee and so on set out on the kitchen table, Douglas," said Sally.

"Thanks," Douglas replied, obviously too busy showing his friends into the dining room to hear what Sally had said.

The Ogre was standing in the doorway of the sitting room with the grim look that he usually reserved for Johnny or Caspar. "I'm beginning to regret this already," he said. "Where *did* Douglas get those awful clothes?"

"I got them for him," said Sally, a trifle guiltily. "He seemed to have grown out of everything else."

"Are they fashionable or something?" asked the Ogre.

"Very," said Sally.

"I feared as much," said the Ogre, and went and turned the television on.

Since the Ogre was clearly in his stormiest mood, Caspar dared not do anything but sit quietly over a map of South America, trying to decide on a geography project. The Ogre gave him several irritated looks, but he said nothing. The television produced the Ogre's favorite kind of program for him—the kind in which Officials and Ministers explained that the country was in a considerable state of crisis, but that they were doing this, that, and the other thing to cure it. Caspar bit back several yawns of boredom and wondered how his mother could stand it. She was calmly checking over some long lists that had to do with her work tomorrow. If Caspar himself had not been in such a pleasant flutter about going flying, he thought he would never have endured it at all.

Indigo Rubber made themselves heard, rather loudly, in the middle of their best song. Caspar raised his head and almost regretted not being in the dining room. Either Douglas's equipment was ten times better than his, or the records had needed cleaning more than he realized. Indigo Rubber sounded superb—though Caspar did wish that one of Douglas's friends had not chosen to pick out the song haltingly on his guitar at the same time.

"This is intolerable!" said the Ogre, and turned the sound on the television right up. The result was a truly awful noise, with a Minister booming away about trade, and Indigo

Rubber gamely competing for all they were worth. "I shall go mad!" said the Ogre, with his face twisted into a snarl.

"No, you won't," said Sally, laughing. "Do turn the sound down. I want to make a list of the people we're having to this party."

The Ogre, typically, refused to turn the sound down. So he and Sally were forced, for the next half hour or so, to bawl names at one another above the noise. Caspar's head began to ache. His mother began to look a little worn also. Luckily, after that, Douglas and his friends took to playing Indigo Rubber songs on their guitars, which, though penetrating, were not quite so loud.

"Shall I send them home?" the Ogre asked several times, but Sally would not hear of it.

"I want to get these invitations out," she said.

"You must be made of iron," said the Ogre eventually. Then he noticed Caspar and told him to go to bed. Caspar was collecting his maps and papers, only too ready to go, when there were voices in the hall, and Douglas burst gaily into the sitting room.

"I say—" he said.

"I'm not going to have you and your noise in here as well," said the Ogre.

Douglas froze into crestfallen politeness. "Sorry, Father. I was only going to ask— You see, my friends are going downtown to the discotheque. Is it all right for me to go, too?"

"No," said the Ogre.

Douglas swallowed, and then said, very patiently and politely, "I shouldn't be more than an hour or so. I promise I'll be back before eleven."

"Which is a good hour past your bedtime," said the Ogre. *"No."*

"Couldn't he go?" said Sally.

"I've already given you my opinion of your indulgence," the Ogre said unpleasantly. "That blasted place is the haunt of half the vice in town."

Caspar felt his stomach twisting and fluttering. It sounded as if Johnny might be going to see some vice after all.

"But all sorts of people go there," Douglas said pleadingly. "My friends often do."

"Then I think the worse of your friends," said the Ogre.

"But they—" began Douglas.

"Absolutely NO!" said the Ogre.

Douglas went out and shut the door quietly behind him. When Caspar went upstairs, he was showing his friends out.

Gwinny and Johnny were asleep, packed into Johnny's bed. Caspar, at the sight, felt rather sleepy himself, but he sat down on his own bed to wait. He heard Douglas come upstairs, and smelled a whiff of chemicals as Douglas opened the door across the landing. After that was a long, long silence. Caspar was all but asleep himself, when Johnny suddenly sat bolt upright.

"What's the time?"

Caspar found the clock, which had got buried under a pile of comics. "Ten-fifteen."

"Oh, good," said Johnny. "I banged my head ten times on the pillow." And he started shaking Gwinny. "Come on. Time to go."

They bustled quietly and excitedly about, getting into warm clothes and putting pillows in their beds. Ten minutes later, they were standing beside the open window, feeling very excited indeed and a little inclined to giggle. Johnny carefully fetched out the almost full tube of chemical and solemnly passed it to Gwinny. Gwinny rolled up the leg of Johnny's old trousers, which she was wearing for warmth, poured the liquid carefully onto her palm, and rubbed it hard on her shin.

"Ooh! It's cold!" she said.

Johnny was just in time to take the test-tube out of her hand as she floated up past him. While he was rubbing the liquid on his leg, Gwinny drummed the ceiling gently with her heels.

"I'd forgotten what a lovely feeling it was," she said.

Caspar was looking up at her when Johnny soared away to join her. He missed his chance of taking the tube and had to climb on the cupboard to take it from Johnny's hand. It all seemed so silly and exciting that they both began laughing.

"Are you boys in bed?" called Sally from below.

"Yes. Just going to sleep," they lied at the tops of their voices. Caspar, still crouching on top of the cupboard, rolled up his trouser-leg. He was quaking so with laughter that he poured far more of the liquid onto his palm than he intended. He splashed the whole ice-cold handful on his leg and, when the delicious lightness spread through him and he, too, floated up to the ceiling, he found he was holding a nearly empty test-tube, with about a quarter of an inch of liquid left in the bottom.

"What shall I do with this?" he said.

"Balance it on the lightshade," suggested Gwinny.

"We ought to put out the light, too," said Johnny.

Caspar, intoxicated with the splendid new feeling of being

light as air, swam himself over to the middle of the room and balanced the test-tube on the lampshade. It was better than swimming. One kick took him yards, with no effort at all. The difficulty came when he tried to reach the light switch. Like Gwinny before, he seemed far heavier upwards than he ever was downwards. He tried jumping off the ceiling in a sort of dive toward the switch, but, no matter how hard he pushed off with his feet, his hand never came within a foot of the switch.

"Why not take the bulb out?" said Johnny, impatient to be off.

So Caspar swam back, put his gloves on, and very carefully took the bulb out without disturbing the test-tube. But as soon as the room went dark, he had no idea where it was any more. He felt his glove brush the shade and the shade tip. Then there was a bump and a slight bursting noise from the floor.

"The tube's fallen off," he said.

"Well, we'd used most of it anyway," said Gwinny. "Do come on."

Caspar put the light bulb in his pocket and swam toward the window. The dark shape of Gwinny first, then Johnny, blotted out the window and soared away upward, as Johnny had done before. There was quite a brisk wind. When Caspar swooped deliciously up past the wall, the gutter, and the glistening roof, he found himself being carried over the roof of the next house toward the center of town. Johnny was floating against the orange glare of the city lights about ten yards ahead, and Gwinny ten yards beyond that and a few feet higher up because she was lighter. The sight gave Caspar a strange, frosty, excited feeling, as if splendid things were about to happen. Being a good swimmer, he caught up with the other two easily.

"How lovely to look down on roofs!" Gwinny said. And indeed it was. The street lights and a good round moon made it all very easy to see. Roofs had all sorts of queer shapes that they would not have expected from the ground. They could look through skylights and see people moving about inside, and television aerials looked surprisingly big when you were beside them.

Another surprising thing was the way bent streets looked straight, and streets they had thought were straight had unexpected little twiddles or long curves to them. They swam themselves merrily over the neighborhood, above wires, roads, gardens, houses, and a park, until they all found that they had no idea where they were.

"Why does it all look so different?" Johnny said crossly.

"The wind's blown us off course," said Caspar. "We'd better find a road we know and follow that, or we'll get lost."

The brightest orange glare seemed now to be away to the right. They swam in that direction, across the wind. It was much harder going. Before long, Gwinny was complaining loudly of being tired.

"Do shut up," Caspar called up at her. "Suppose someone hears you and tells the police." He was fairly tired himself by this time. The feeling of frosty excitement he had first had seemed entirely to have gone. He was hot and worried. The only thing that stopped him suggesting that they go home was that it seemed so tame. But the fact was that one empty, dark street is much like another, and merely flying across them stops being fun after a while.

"Let's rest," said Johnny.

They anchored themselves to a convenient television aerial and floated, panting. Beneath them, on a corner, was a pub with people noisily coming out of it.

"There's some vice for you, Johnny," said Caspar, as a very fat man rolled to the edge of the pavement and stood there singing. Gwinny laughed, because he was so fat she could not see his feet. Johnny watched him dubiously. The fat man stopped singing and began to shout rude remarks at imaginary people across the road.

"That's not vice," said Johnny. "He's drunk."

"Do you know," said Gwinny, "this is the pub on the corner near where we used to live! I know that fat man. He's the greengrocer who gave me the wrong change. We can't be far off Market Street. Yes, look." She pointed a glove toward a big block of buildings towering against the orange glare. "That's the Ogre's office. I met him quite near there, so I know if we go past it, Market Street is only over some roofs."

"So it is!" said Johnny, and Caspar felt foolish at not having recognized it long before.

So they set off toward the building, across the wind again, using television aerials to push off from. Each aerial bent and twanged as they used it, until the streets behind them hummed. Then they pushed off in a long swoop across a little dark space like a chasm and were able to pull themselves hand over hand along the towering side of the office-block. All its lights were on. They handed themselves across a window that could well have belonged to the Ogre's office. Inside were typewriters with covers on them, and not very comfortable-looking desks and chairs.

"It's a bit like school," said Gwinny. "I shan't work in an office when I grow up."

"I can't think how the Ogre can bear to," said Johnny. "I suppose it's because he's not human."

They dived off from the office-block across some tall, steep roofs, which were almost too high for them to get over, and there they were at last, at the end of Market Street. And that was splendid from the air. Colored street signs flashed on and off, people hurried, shops shone, and cars went in lines down the middle, so close together that, as Johnny said, they looked from above like a train someone had chopped into bits. A nice rowdy noise came up, and petrol fumes made Caspar sneeze. The Christmas lights were the only disappointing part. From the air, they seemed to be all scaffolding and wires, with a bit of a glitter below, almost out of sight.

"They're made to be seen from the ground," said Caspar.

They worked their way down the street, almost in the teeth of the wind. It was very slow going, even using parapets and dormer windows to push off from, and Caspar could not help being a little nervous of all the electric wires strung across the street. They passed the discotheque on the other side of the road. Caspar recognized it from the big red, lighted disc outside and the sound of muffled music.

"Douglas wanted to go there with his friends tonight, but the Ogre wouldn't let him," he told the others.

They were not surprised. After that, they stopped and roosted on the arch over the Town Hall, where a number of pigeons, frightened and offended, flapped away from their floating feet. Here Johnny thought he saw some vice. There was a group of youths just below, laughing and shouting and twanging guitars.

"No, those are only Douglas's friends," said Caspar. "I suppose they're going home from the discotheque."

"I almost think the Ogre was right for once," Gwinny said severely. "Those friends look loud and rough."

"They're just old," said Caspar.

"And I bet the Ogre was just being his own mean, Ogrish self," said Johnny. "Wasn't he, Caspar?"

"Let's go home," said Caspar. He suddenly thought what the Ogre might say and do to them, if he discovered they had been to Market Street, and the idea made him notice that he was cold and very tired. Johnny and Gwinny felt much the same. They set off again down Market Street.

They had almost reached the roundabout at the end, when Gwinny squawked, clapped her hand over her mouth, and pointed across the street. The boys looked. And they were so astonished at what they saw that they stopped swimming and stared, and the wind carried all three of them back up the street again.

On the other side of Market Street, about ten feet lower down than they were, swam a sort of aerial frogman. He was whipping along, face downward, past lighted windows and over people's heads, with his hands by his sides and the great black flippers on his feet wagging away steadily.

"Oh-oh, they've landed!" said Johnny. It was the first thought in all their minds. But, as the figure came abreast of a street light, they saw it was Douglas, with the hood of his anorak up and wearing flippers. They all secretly thought the flippers were a very good idea, and wished they had thought of them, too. "They've found the flying-powder, too," said Johnny.

"And he's using it to go to the discotheque," said Caspar, rather awed at Douglas's daring. "He's late. He's missed the others."

"Let's follow him," said Gwinny. "Then we can drop dark hints about where he went."

"And get him scared silly we'll tell the Ogre," said Johnny. "Aha! Little does he know we have him in our power!"

Chuckling at this extremely pleasant thought, they all set off up Market Street again as hard as they could go. The wind behind them helped, but Douglas, also with the wind behind him and the flippers in addition, drew steadily ahead. No matter how hard they shunted themselves from windows and balconies, they were nowhere near him when he reached the discotheque. But, to their great surprise, Douglas shot straight past, over the big red disc and on up the street.

"I suppose he'll have to wait for it to wear off and land somewhere secret," Caspar suggested as a possible explanation.

Even so, it was odd that the now distant figure of Douglas should then cross, flippering steadily, over the traffic and continue up Market Street on the same side as they were. They hastened after him, but by the time they reached the Market Cross Hotel, they had lost him completely.

"He's probably down by now," Johnny said crossly.

Gwinny anchored herself to the scaffolding above the *K* of the big blue hotel sign and refused to go on. "I'm tired," she said, floating out from the bar as she might in a swimming pool.

"Don't touch that!" said Caspar. "You'll get an electric shock."

"And probably put out all the street lights, too," said Johnny.

"I don't care," said Gwinny. "I'm so tired I could die."

Johnny suddenly clutched at the scaffolding, too, just above the *E*.

"Johnny!" said Caspar.

"I'm going heavy!" said Johnny.

"Oh, so am I!" gasped Gwinny. "Caspar, what shall we do?"

Chapter 5

I t was one of the most horrible moments Caspar had
known. He was perfectly sure that if either Johnny or
Gwinny put their feet as well as their hands on the scaffold and completed the circuit, they could get an electric shock
strong enough to kill them. But now they could not let go. He
was not going heavy himself. He thought, because of the way
he had been laughing, he had put rather more flying potion on
than the others. But it was obviously only a matter of minutes
before that wore off, too.

"Keep your feet off that thing!" he said to Johnny, and
grabbed Gwinny round the waist. Behind the scaffold and the
lighted lettering was a narrow ledge, which ran along the front
of the hotel between two rows of windows. It looked about
wide enough to take their feet. Caspar swam upwind, crabwise,
to it, holding Gwinny clutched against him. She felt as heavy as
lead. He managed to turn her round and push her onto the
ledge, with her back against the wall of the hotel.

"Now don't dare move!" he said, and swam back for
Johnny. Johnny was lashing his feet frantically, trying to use
the last of his lightness to keep them clear of the scaffold.
Caspar had to come at him sideways and grab him round the
neck. By the time they reached the ledge, Johnny was making

throttled noises and could only gasp and lean.

Then Caspar felt himself going heavy. He only had just time to turn round and back against the wall of the hotel before the potion left him, and he went down on the ledge with a thump so heavy that he nearly overbalanced and fell off. It would have been a real fall, too, all the way down to the street. The distance they were above ground, which had been exciting such a short time ago, now seemed appalling. Caspar shut his eyes and sweated.

"What shall we do?" said Gwinny. "Shout for help?"

There were still crowds of people passing below, but they dared not bend their heads to look at them.

"Don't be a fool!" said Johnny. "We'll get taken to a police station, and the next thing we know, the Ogre will be interrogating us in person." He tried turning his head up to see how far they were away from the row of windows above, and nearly overbalanced. On top of clinging to the wall, this was too much for him. His knees shook, and he felt giddy.

"Caspar, what shall we do?" said Gwinny.

"I think we'd better wait and see if Douglas comes back," said Caspar.

"Oh no! Not him!" Johnny said faintly.

"But you said he'd come down by now," protested Gwinny. "And if he walks past underneath us, we won't see him. And if he goes on the other side of the road, he won't hear us. Besides, what good could he do?"

"I don't know," said Caspar. "But it's all I can think of."

"I hate him," objected Johnny.

"He's about the only person in the world who'll understand what's happened," said Caspar. "Except Malcolm, I suppose."

"I hate him worse," said Johnny.

Nevertheless, they settled down to wait. The gay street twinkled and roared around them. The Christmas lights glittered. Street signs winked on and off. People talked below, and laughed, and someone in the hotel played a piano rather badly. And solitary and unseen and stiff as statues, the three children stood on the ledge and waited, more hopelessly with every minute that passed.

They were so tired and miserable that they nearly missed Douglas when he came. He flashed flippering past, just below the ledge and the hotel sign. He was in front of *CROSS* before they saw him, nearly too far away to hear their urgent whispers.

"Douglas!" they all hissed desperately.

Douglas's flippers faltered, and then began to move faster. Johnny risked shouting.

"DOUGLAS!"

With a swirl of flippers, Douglas stopped himself by hanging onto the scaffolding, just below the first *T,* and turned to see who was shouting. When he saw it was them, he shrugged his shoulders and was obviously about to flipper away again.

"Please," Gwinny called imploringly.

Slowly and grudgingly, Douglas handed himself back along the letters, until he was hanging on below the *L,* looking up at them. He did not look in the least friendly. "All right," he said. "So we've discovered the flying-powder, too. If you wanted to keep it secret, you shouldn't have made such a darned fuss getting Gwinny off the ceiling."

"So you did see her?" said Caspar.

"Yes. Do you want to make anything of it?" Douglas inquired unpleasantly.

"No," said Gwinny. "Douglas, we've all gone heavy."

There was a silence full of town noises, during which Douglas looked thoroughly exasperated.

"And we're stuck here," explained Johnny.

"Just like you were on the side of the house. I know," said Douglas. "What do you expect me to do about it? How much powder have you left?"

"None, I'm afraid," said Caspar. "The last bit fell off the light as we were leaving."

"Oh, trust you stupid little squits to get yourselves into a mess!" said Douglas. "It's just *typical*. All right, I'll go and get you some of ours, but you'll have to wait. I've got to see to Malcolm first. He's in even more of a mess than you are." So saying, Douglas, with a deft swirl of flippers, pushed off from the *L*, and shot away among the other street signs.

Now that they had some hope of rescue, waiting was easier. But nothing could make standing perilously on that narrow ledge pleasant. Johnny's feet went numb, and he was forced to shift cautiously from foot to foot.

"Keep still," said Caspar. "You'll knock us all off."

"I can't help it," said Johnny.

Gwinny suddenly broke into song. "Abide with me. Fast falls the something sky."

"Eh?" said Johnny.

"Shut *up*!" said Caspar.

"I was singing to keep our spirits up," explained Gwinny.

"Well, stop," said Caspar. "You'll have the hotel manager up instead, and he'll get the fire brigade and we'll end up in no end of trouble. And just think how mad Douglas will be if he comes all the way back here for nothing."

This caused them all to stand silently for a while. Then Johnny said, "What was Douglas doing then, if he wasn't going to the discotheque?"

"Something to do with the mess Malcolm's in?" Gwinny suggested.

Caspar said nothing. He was secretly rather disappointed that Douglas had not defied the Ogre after all.

"Yes, what mess *is* he in?" wondered Johnny. "If he's gone heavy somewhere peculiar, Douglas wouldn't need to come here, would he?"

"If they've discovered the powder, too, that explains the sweater on the chimney," said Gwinny. "It was them."

"Trust them to keep quiet and let us take the blame!" said Johnny.

But even this topic wore out after a time. They stood in a stiff row, while the street noises died away beneath. The piano in the hotel stopped, and the roar of cars decreased until it was only occasional. Then there seemed to be no more cars and just one or two heavy lorries. The pavement they could see across the road was empty. A few solitary people walked in or out of the hotel below, but that was all. The street signs went out, one by one, though the Christmas lights still twinkled gaily on a level with their heads. And the hotel sign stayed alight, coloring all their faces a ghastly blue. The color just expressed the way they were feeling by then. They were cold, miserable, and tired, and each of them suspected that Douglas had gone home and forgotten all about them.

They must have waited a good hour before Douglas

arrived. Market Street was so quiet by then that they heard him panting before they saw him, and the slapping, whistling noise the flippers made. Never had any noise been more welcome. They craned forward. Douglas was coming, flippering vigorously, under the hotel sign, some three feet lower than he had been. When he reached the letter *L,* they saw that it took him a considerable effort to heave himself up so that he could get a grip on the scaffold, and when he had hold of it he was hanging more than floating.

"Thank you awfully for coming," Caspar said.

Douglas, in reply, held up a test-tube with a cork in it. It was just over half-full of liquid. "Here you are," he said, rather breathlessly. "That's our last drop and you're each to use a quarter of it. Then give it back to me, because I need it to get home on."

Gwinny, with great difficulty, managed to bend her knees sufficiently to reach the tube. "It is kind of you," she said.

"Oh, don't madden me by being grateful," said Douglas. "Get on and use it. And hurry up. I go heavy awfully quickly."

Gwinny hastily uncorked the tube and poured a quarter— or perhaps less, because she was so dismayed at what Douglas said—of the liquid into her hand.

"Rub it on anywhere," said Douglas. "Your face'll do. And make sure Johnny's got the tube first."

So Gwinny handed the test-tube to Johnny and splashed the icy handful of liquid onto her cheeks. The feeling of lightness spread through her, and her feet gently left the ledge. Douglas startled her by reaching up and grabbing hold of her ankle.

"Hang on to me," he said. "You can help hold me up."

While Johnny was measuring out his quarter and passing the tube to Caspar, Gwinny struggled her way down Douglas's outstretched arm and twisted her fingers into his anorak. His weight brought her down a little, and they both floated just below the big blue *L*. Then Johnny bobbed clear of the ledge.

"Catch hold of Gwinny," said Douglas. "And you," he said to Caspar, "keep that tube and pass it down the line to me."

Caspar, though he was a little annoyed at being ordered about and organized like this, did as he was told. As soon as he was floating, he caught hold of Johnny. The tube traveled slowly and perilously down to Gwinny, who poured the last small quantity down into Douglas's cupped hand. Douglas gave a sigh of relief and splashed it on his face.

"Right," he said. "Keep hanging on and all kick like mad. And let's hope we've got enough to get us home. If we haven't, there'll be hell to pay. Father was prowling round the house really suspiciously when I left."

With these encouraging words, he let go the letter *L* and at once sank about three feet lower. They floated in an irregular ballooning line, with Johnny highest, clutching Gwinny's scarf. Douglas's flippers beat, and they felt themselves tugged down Market Street. They all kicked too, Gwinny like a frog, the boys in imitation of Douglas. They gathered momentum as they kicked, and shortly they were going very well indeed— almost ten miles an hour, Johnny reckoned breathlessly. They flashed down Market Street, drove across the roundabout and, panting hard, kicked their way through the zigzag of streets toward home. They were halfway up their own street when Gwinny felt Douglas dropping.

"Oh dear!" she said.

"Faster," said Douglas. "Kick like mad, all of you."

They kicked frantically, dropping lower and lower, until Caspar's feet were almost pointing upward. Douglas was trailing down, brushing people's hedges. About two houses off their own, he went finally and completely heavy. All four dropped downward, trailing like a kite's tail, and Douglas, with all his weight dangling from Gwinny's fingers, was dragged across the pavement on the ends of his flippers.

"Oh!" squeaked Gwinny. "I can't! I can't hold on!"

"You've got to," said Caspar. "Kick, Johnny."

By kicking violently, they trailed Douglas ten yards. Gwinny was squeaking all the time that she could not hold on, and with every kick they all sank lower and lower.

"This is no good," said Douglas. "You'll have to let go." He braced his flippers and stood still, with them hanging upward from him, so that Caspar's heels were level with the nearest street light. "Let go," said Douglas. "I'll have to climb in through the kitchen window."

"That's not fair," said Gwinny. "Suppose you get caught?"

"I won't, with luck," said Douglas. "Go on, let go, before you go heavy, too. If we all have to climb in, we're bound to be caught. Let go, and get up to our window—I left it open."

"I'll come down and open the kitchen window for you, shall I?" Caspar offered.

"And get me caught? I know you," said Douglas. "Just get in and get to bed and don't make any blasted *noise* for once. Go on."

Since he really seemed to mean it, and sounded rather like the Ogre as he said it, Gwinny untwisted her fingers from his anorak and let go. The three of them floated upward, past the level of the street light, and almost as high as the curtained slit of light at the front of their house where Douglas's open window was.

"Good luck," Gwinny said.

Douglas looked up at them rather contemptuously, as Caspar took the lead and began to trail them toward the window. "Get a move on," he said.

It was as well they went when they did. Gwinny went heavy as Caspar put out his hand and grasped the windowsill. With a muffled, whispering struggle, he and Johnny hauled her up and thrust her through the window between the curtains. Johnny went heavy on the windowsill, and Caspar as he reached the table just below the window. They all crouched breathlessly on this table, blinking in the light and looking round a room they had scarcely ever seen before.

The room was much the same size as Johnny's and Caspar's, though it was a different shape. But it seemed far bigger, because it was scrupulously tidy. Books were in the bookcase and Douglas's guitar tidily against the wall. Other things were neatly arranged in a glass-fronted cupboard. Douglas's bed was unwrinkled. The bed in which Malcolm was asleep was equally free of wrinkles. The only things out of place were the chemistry set open in the middle of the floor, and a great deal of dust everywhere.

"What's the matter?" Malcolm demanded pettishly. "Where's Douglas?"

They stared round the room and then at one another. The sleeping shape in Malcolm's bed had not moved, and yet Malcolm's voice had come from the region of Douglas's bed, on the opposite side of the room.

"He went heavy in the road," Gwinny said to the sleeping hump, wondering if Malcolm was secretly a ventriloquist. "He told us to come in without him."

"Oh *no!*" said Malcolm, and again his voice came from the wrong place. "If you've got him caught, I shan't ever forgive you!"

There was a shuffling noise from under Douglas's bed, and Malcolm walked out from underneath it. Their eyes popped. He was about a foot high. All of him was small in proportion, except that perhaps his head was a little too big for his body. He had no clothes on. Instead, he was wrapped in a shirt, which he was clutching round him like a cloak, and which trailed behind and around him, making a shiny path on the dusty floor. They could see Malcolm's tiny hands each grasping a shirt button, and they stared in amazement at his equally tiny toes.

Malcolm shivered. "At least shut the window, can't you!" he said, with dignity.

Johnny, quite overawed, turned round and clapped the window shut. Gwinny looked across at the hump in Malcolm's bed, rather ashamed. She could see it was only a pillow now.

"However did you get like that?" said Caspar.

"In the cause of science," Malcolm said haughtily. "Didn't Douglas tell you? I was much smaller than this at bedtime. It took ages to climb out of my clothes, and then I couldn't get Douglas to hear me, let alone see me."

"But what did you do?" said Johnny. "What did it?"

"It's a tube called *Parv. Pulv.,*" said Malcolm, "and I advise you not to fool about with it. It's rather awful being that small. The grains of dust look as big as footballs. And I kept being blown over in the draft under the door. All I did was sniff it."

"Wow!" said Johnny, quite appalled to think that he might have been in the same case any time that week.

"But what made Douglas have to go into town?" asked Gwinny.

"To find out the antidote, of course," said Malcolm. "The sets came from a toy shop near Father's office, and we didn't dare try anything else in case I vanished completely. The old boy was watching telly, and Douglas said he was furious at being disturbed."

"But he told you the antidote?" Caspar said.

"Yes. It's *Magn. Pulv.,*" said Malcolm. "I thought that was magnesium. But it works—though I seem to be growing awfully slowly," he complained, looking down at his pigmy body with distaste. "What's Douglas doing?"

"What will you do if you're not the right size for school tomorrow?" Gwinny asked, with interest.

"I don't know," Malcolm said crossly. "*You* tell me."

"Perhaps you should have some more of the antidote?" Johnny suggested.

Malcolm shuddered. "*No!* I had to eat a whole grain, and it tastes horrible. What's Douglas doing? How is he going to get in?"

"But how much did the old man tell you to eat?" Johnny persisted.

"He didn't," said Malcolm. "He just said it was *Magn. Pulv.* Where's Douglas?"

"Then perhaps you should wash in it," said Gwinny.

"Climbing in through the kitchen window," said Caspar.

"Well!" said Malcolm. "I think the least you could do was go down and open it for him."

"He wouldn't let me," said Caspar. "I offered. I'm not a complete brute, whatever you think."

Malcolm gathered the shirt around him and trailed with dignity toward the door. "Can I trouble you to turn the handle?" he said coldly. "I see I shall have to go down and try to open the darn thing myself."

"How can you that size?" Johnny said, climbing off the table. "Don't be a fool. I'll go. It had better be me," he explained to the other two. "The Ogre thinks I'm capable of any crime anyway, and I can always say I was stealing biscuits."

Malcolm swung round from the door. "Who are you calling an ogre?"

"Your flipping father," said Caspar. "And you know he is, so don't argue."

"I know no such thing," Malcolm said uncertainly.

"I'd better go down and see, anyway," Johnny said. Since Malcolm was in his way, he picked him up, moderately gently, and put him to one side of the door. Malcolm stuttered with indignation, but he was helpless. Johnny opened the door and crept heavily out onto the landing, into the remnant of old chemical smells.

Before he had reached the head of the stairs, the whole house echoed with a shattering crash. Johnny froze. So did Malcolm in the doorway. Gwinny, who was in the middle of the room with Caspar, covered her ears and held her breath. Caspar, with horrible clarity, remembered the big jug of orange juice which had been on the kitchen windowsill that evening.

Light was snapped on below. Heavy footsteps hurried. Gwinny and Caspar found themselves out on the landing with Johnny, and Malcolm came scuttling between them.

There was a long, awful silence. Then the Ogre's voice was raised in a perfect roar:

"You disobedient little devil!"

After that, the Ogre's voice rumbled and roared, on and on, for what seemed hours, accusing Douglas of going to the discotheque when he had been told not to, and of other crimes besides. Caspar, Johnny and Gwinny all felt sick. They did not need Malcolm to say, between chattering teeth, *"Now look what you've done!"* to remind them that it was their fault Douglas was caught like this. And to make matters worse, Douglas plainly could not think what to say. For a long time, there was no sound from him at all. Then his voice was raised in a faint-sounding denial.

The Ogre shouted, *"And don't give me those lies!"* There was the sound of a heavy blow falling. And another. All four on the landing winced each time.

A door opened downstairs. Sally's voice said, "Jack! Really—!"

"Will you kindly allow me to deal with this as I think best," said the Ogre.

There was no reply. The door shut again. After that, the Ogre roared on again, and there were sounds that suggested Douglas was having to clear up the jug and the orange juice that had been in it. Then there was still more shouting, until they could hardly bear it, which at last died away to a rumble, followed by silence. They sighed. Johnny looked toward Malcolm and found he had grown. His head was now level with Gwinny's shoulder.

They all looked anxiously toward the stairs again. They could hear Douglas coming up two at a time. The light came on at their landing, showing Malcolm now nearly Gwinny's size and looking a little indecent in just a shirt. Then Douglas came galloping upwards with such an expression of fury and misery on his face that Caspar braced himself to run and Gwinny and Johnny backed away.

Douglas halted on the top stair when he saw the four of them on the landing. "Flaming pustules!" he said. "There's no privacy in this blessed house!" He turned round and went galloping downstairs again. They heard the bathroom door slam and the bolt lock with a shriek.

Then the Ogre's heavy feet began marching up the stairs.

"Quick!" whispered Caspar to Malcolm. "Don't let him see you that size!" He and Johnny took Malcolm and hurled him into his room, and Malcolm did not protest. Gwinny raced upstairs to her room. Caspar and Johnny fled to theirs, tore off their clothes, and dived into bed. When the Ogre arrived in their doorway, they were both between surprisingly cold sheets, breathing as heavily and slowly as they could. The Ogre clicked their light switch, muttered a little when the light would not come on, and went across the landing to see what Malcolm was doing. Whatever he saw there seemed to satisfy him, for he went heavily away downstairs.

Caspar waited until his bedroom door shut. Then he got up again and put on his pajamas, closed the window, and dug the light bulb out of his coat pocket. When he had succeeded in putting it back in its socket, he discovered, considerably to his surprise, that Johnny was asleep. Caspar felt fairly sleepy himself, but he knew he could not possibly go to sleep without a word at least of apology and thanks to Douglas. So he went out and sat on the landing to wait for him.

He was nine-tenths asleep, with his forehead on his knees, when he heard his mother's voice on the landing below. "Douglas," she was saying. "Douglas, please won't you come out?" Caspar could tell she was just outside the bathroom door. After she had called again several times, he heard Douglas's voice. He could not hear what Douglas said, but it sounded like a gruff refusal. "Oh, come on, Douglas," Sally said. "How would it be if I made you some cocoa?" There was a further mutter from Douglas. It sounded less gruff. Caspar was glad. He knew that if it had been him in the bathroom, he would have wanted cocoa, and comfort, too.

But before Sally could speak again, Caspar heard the voice of the Ogre. "Sally, for heaven's sake come back to bed. I'll deal with the stupid little fool." And then he heard the Ogre's fist pound on the bathroom door. "Douglas," said the Ogre, "come on out of there and stop behaving like a spoiled baby. If you don't come out this instant, it'll be the worse for you when you do."

"Look, Jack—" said Sally.

"Shut up," said the Ogre. "Did you hear me, Douglas?"

"Yes, I heard you," said the muffled, sulky voice of Douglas. The bolt clicked. Caspar heard the door open.

"Now get to bed," said the Ogre savagely. "I've had about enough of you."

Douglas came swiftly upstairs. Caspar, rather nervously, stood up. Douglas stopped when he saw him.

"I wanted to say sorry," Caspar whispered.

But Douglas was in no mood for apologies. "You wait!" he said, in a furious low rumble. "I owe you for this. You just wait!"

Chapter 6

Although Malcolm was his own size again the next morning, everyone, not surprisingly, was torpid and tired. Johnny staggered from his bed and went to school without really waking up. Both Caspar and Malcolm arrived late and had to stand publicly at the back of assembly. Douglas left the house when the Ogre and Sally did, which meant that he must have been late also, but since he went to the senior school, no one knew what had happened. Gwinny fared best because the Ogre, seeing she was going to be late, took her down to juniors in his car.

After school, Johnny as usual managed to get home first. He pelted up to their room and there, in spite of a sudden overwhelming desire to roll on his bed and go to sleep, he doggedly sorted through the crowded and disorderly chemistry box until he had found the two tubes marked *Parv. Pulv.* and *Magn. Pulv.* His idea was to tape them together and then stick a label on them saying DANGER. But once he had them in his hand, it occurred to him to experiment. After all, he had the antidote ready.

Caspar also sped home, with an understandable desire to be out of sight when Douglas arrived. He reached the door of their room to see Johnny holding the tube to his nose and sniffing raucously. Johnny, hearing him, looked up guiltily.

"I'm only experimenting," he said to Caspar's accusing face. "And I think Malcolm was lying. That was my third sniff."

Since the damage seemed to be done, Caspar could only wait. They waited tensely, expecting Johnny to become a Johnny-shaped speck any moment. But nothing happened. In five minutes, Johnny underwent no change at all—except from guilt to annoyance.

"You see!" he said disgustedly. "You can't believe a word Malcolm says."

"What do you think he did do?" Caspar said.

They heard Malcolm himself coming upstairs just then, trailing wearily from step to step. They looked at one another and had the same idea at the same moment. Without needing to exchange a word, they got up, crept to the open door, and waited on either side of it out of sight. The moment Malcolm passed the top stair and his shadow fell through the doorway, they darted out and pounced. There was a squalling, indignant struggle, and they got him into their room. Johnny shut the door and stood with his back to it. Caspar took hold of Malcolm and pinned him by the upper arms against the wall.

"What do you want?" said Malcolm. "Let go, can't you!"

"When you come clean," said Caspar. "What did you really do with *Parv. Pulv.*?"

"I don't know. I'm tired. Let go," said Malcolm.

"Not until you tell us," said Johnny.

"What makes you think I'm going to tell you?" countered Malcolm.

"Because we won't let you go until you do," said Caspar.

There was a short time of deadlock. Malcolm leaned defiantly against the wall, and Caspar leaned on his arms to hold him there and wondered what he could do to scare Malcolm into confessing. Then Malcolm said, with great loftiness, "You wouldn't understand if I did tell you. You've no idea of system, or controlling your experiments, or even keeping your ideas in order. All you do is muddle about and hope. It's no wonder you haven't made the discoveries that I have. I bet you didn't even realize that it's always the things on the lower layer that are odd. But I've come to that conclusion, because I'm systematic."

This exasperated Johnny and Caspar. They saw well enough that Malcolm had no intention of telling them what he had done with *Parv. Pulv.* and was just trying to distract their attention.

"Stop waffling," said Johnny, "and tell us."

"Can you see any reason," said Malcolm, "why I should share my discoveries with you, Melchior?"

Johnny, to be quite honest, could see no reason at all. Which meant that Caspar was forced to say, "Because we're going to make you tell us. What have you found out?"

"Nothing I'm going to tell you," said Malcolm.

Caspar lifted Malcolm away from the wall and banged him back, so that his irritatingly tidy head thumped against the plaster. "What other chemicals do things?" he asked menacingly.

At that moment, Douglas, outside on the landing, said, "Hey, Malcolm!"

Caspar and Johnny both jumped, because they had not heard Douglas come upstairs. Malcolm looked at Caspar, coolly and jeeringly, and Caspar looked back, daring Malcolm to shout for help.

"Malcolm?" said Douglas again. They waited tensely while Douglas went into the room across the landing and came out again. Then Douglas said, "Oh drat!" and went galloping away downstairs. As soon as he had gone, Caspar felt suddenly tired to death of the whole matter. He wanted to yawn in Malcolm's face. Instead, he let go of him. Malcolm, with dignity, straightened his tie and went toward the door.

But Johnny at that moment thought of a very good reason why Malcolm should share at least one discovery with them. "You tell us about *Parv. Pulv.*," he said. "You'd never have known anything could happen at all, if Douglas hadn't seen Gwinny flying." And he did not move from in front of the door.

Malcolm stopped. There was not so much difference between his size and Johnny's, and Johnny was burly. "I dare say we'd have worked it out," he said loftily.

"Yes. *We*," said Johnny. "Don't pretend Douglas isn't helping you."

"So what?" said Malcolm. "Don't tell me you're working entirely alone, Melchior. And there are three of you."

"But Douglas is older," said Johnny. "So it's not fair."

"Your ages add up to more than ours," said Malcolm.

Caspar felt more tired than ever. "Oh, let him go, Johnny," he said. "This is boring."

Johnny moved reluctantly aside. Malcolm swiftly got his hand to the doorknob. Then he said, "I don't see I've any call to tell you anything. I bet you only discovered the flying powder by mistake and spilled it on Gwinny by accident."

The mortifying thing was that this was quite true. As Malcolm slipped round the door, Johnny said angrily, "You wait. I'll discover something you've never dreamt of. You needn't think you're so clever." Malcolm shut the door in his face with a bang. Johnny turned round and ploughed feverishly through the construction kits to the chemistry set. He threw himself down beside it and began to scrabble among the comics and toffee-bars around it. "The instructions," he said. "Have you seen the instructions, Caspar?"

"No. Why?" said Caspar, yawning.

"I've *got* to find out which tubes were on the bottom layer," Johnny said desperately. "I've got them all mixed up."

Caspar saw reason in this. They searched fiercely. Johnny found the broken test-tube that had held the flying mixture and cut his finger on it. Caspar found nothing but toffee-bars and comics, until he thought to lift up the lid of the chemistry set. The outside of it said *Magicator Chemistry by Magicraft. Guaranteed nontoxic, nonexplosive.* The inside of the lid said the same, but underneath that were instructions of a sort. Caspar read, *1. Try this experiment with Marble Chips.* "These are no good," he said. "I did all these at school."

"No, you fool!" said Johnny, sucking his bleeding finger. "Under your knee."

Caspar seized the little pamphlet he was kneeling on. *Magicator Chemistry,* it said. But it turned out to be a set of quite ordinary experiments, all of which either he or Johnny had done at school. And nowhere did it give a list of the substances in the set. "This is no good, either," he said, smothering a yawn.

"All right," Johnny said grimly. "I'll just have to go through and test each one. I'm not going to be beaten by that stuck-up toff, so there!"

By suppertime, he had sorted out the chemicals he knew, but by then he was too tired to go on. He was only too glad to trudge downstairs and sit round the table with four other people as tired as he was.

"Good gracious!" said Sally, looking round at their white faces and reddened eyes. She knew there was every reason why Douglas should be heavy-eyed and morose, but she could not understand the rest of them. "I hope you're not all sickening with something."

"Only sickening in the other sense," said the Ogre, with his usual uncanny instinct for wrongdoing. "They were fooling about half the night, that was all."

"Oh no, Father, I think I really am coming down with something," Malcolm said coolly. "I have a heavy feeling in my head."

"Serves you right," said the Ogre.

"And I think there must be something wrong with me, too," Gwinny said hastily, "because I'm so quiet."

"Please don't apologize," said the Ogre politely. "It's such a welcome change."

The meal finished in silence both weary and nervous. Though the Ogre said nothing more, Caspar could not help keeping an anxious eye on Douglas. He was even more nervous of him than of the Ogre. When he found Douglas morosely waiting in the hall after supper, it took him some courage not to run away. But all Douglas did was to thrust the Indigo Rubber records at him.

"They're clean now," he said. "Mind you keep them that

way." Then he went away upstairs. Caspar, hardly able to believe his good fortune, stood clutching the records and looking after him uncertainly. Douglas leaned down over the banister. "I haven't forgotten I owe you," he said. "If I could keep my eyes open I'd give it to you now."

It was surprising how ready everyone was for bed that night. By nine o'clock, thick silence had fallen on the house. Caspar was just dropping off to sleep, thinking that he was going to get an all-time low mark on tomorrow's French test, when Johnny said, irritably and drowsily, "Do you think Malcolm was lying about the things in the bottom layer?"

Caspar wanted to go to sleep so badly that he said, "I'll get it out of him tomorrow—if you shut up and don't say another word."

It was a rash promise. Johnny held him to it the next morning. "I did my bit," he said. "I *didn't* say a word—and I lay awake for nearly a quarter of an hour worrying. Now you go and talk to Malcolm." Then, seeing how reluctant Caspar was, he added, "Or I won't tell you a single thing I discover. Ever."

"Oh, all right!" Caspar said crossly. And, as they heard Douglas bounding downstairs at that moment, he went across the landing there and then.

The door was ajar. Caspar opened the hostilities by doing as Malcolm always did—knocking and going in without waiting for an answer. Malcolm was tying his tie in front of the mirror. Caspar, who rarely looked in a mirror if he could help it, and especially not to tie his tie, felt very scornful.

"What do you want?" said Malcolm.

"Information," said Caspar. "Were you lying about the

things on the bottom layer or not?"

"No," said Malcolm, and, as he tightened the knot of his tie, he whistled, gently and mockingly, "We Three Kings of Orient Are."

Caspar of course perceived the insult. "Then, if you weren't, prove it," he said.

"Why?" said Malcolm, and pursed his lips to whistle again.

"Whistle that again and I'll knock your head off!" snarled Caspar.

Malcolm smiled maliciously. "Why not, Capsule?"

"And don't call me that, either!"

"It suits you. Everyone knows you're a perfect pill," said Malcolm. Then, just before Caspar had time to explode, he went on patronizingly, "I've no objection to proving it, since you're obviously too stupid to work it out for yourself."

"Go on then," said Caspar.

Malcolm left the mirror and opened the glass cupboard, where the chemistry set was neatly laid on a shelf. "See?" he said, lifting the lid. "These are all things we've heard of. But underneath," he said, lifting off the first layer and revealing the second, "you've got things even Douglas has never heard of. And most of them don't react in ordinary tests. Do you follow me?"

"Yes, teacher," said Caspar. "What does that prove?"

"Well, you don't think I'm going to test one for you now, before breakfast, do you?" demanded Malcolm.

"Yes," said Caspar.

"Well, I'm not," said Malcolm.

"So you were lying? I thought you were," said Caspar.

"I was *not*!" said Malcolm. "All right. Which one shall I test?"

"This one," said Caspar, pointing to a bottle labeled *Animal Spirits.*

"That's a boring one," said Malcolm. "Nothing happens, even when you taste it, except you feel rather lively for a bit. What about this one?" He picked up a slender tube called, as far as Caspar could see, *Misc. Pulv.*

"What about it?" Caspar said suspiciously.

"I don't know," said Malcolm. "I've done everything I can think of with it, and nothing's happened. The only thing I haven't done is taste it."

"Taste it!" said Caspar. "Suppose it's poison!"

"It says nontoxic," Malcolm said coolly. "I'm willing to taste it, if you'll agree to taste it, too." He looked patronizingly at Caspar, as if he knew Caspar would not dare.

Caspar thought he saw his game. "If you think you're going to get out of it that way, you're making a big mistake," he said. "All right. Let's both taste it."

It was clear Malcolm had hoped to get out of it. He uncorked the tube most unwillingly and said, "It's going to taste pretty nasty, I think."

"Hard luck," said Caspar. "Hand some over."

Malcolm carefully picked up a little glass shovel and spooned a small quantity of white powder out of the tube and onto Caspar's palm. Caspar could not help being impressed with the difference between this care and Johnny's slapdash methods. Then the smell of the powder met his nostrils.

"Eeughk!" he said.

"That's why I didn't taste it," said Malcolm, shoveling the powder onto his own palm. He carefully recorked the tube and put it and the little shovel down. "So if neither of us wants any breakfast, it'll be your fault. Ready?"

"Ready," said Caspar, daunted but determined. They both watched one another like cats for any sign of weakness—and of course both would have died rather than show any—as they each raised a stinking hand to his mouth, put out a reluctant tongue, and licked up a mouthful of what was certainly the nastiest taste Caspar had ever come across. The eyes of both watered. It was stronger than onions and bitterer than gall. Both trying to conceal their shudders, they swallowed.

The result was the most curious whirling, dizzy, sick feeling. Caspar had to shut his eyes. He felt as if he were being taken up by a small whirlwind and put down facing the other way. Fighting not to be sick, he opened his eyes and stared at the white face opposite him. Then he shut his eyes again, opened them, and stared with unbelieving horror. Though he did not often look in mirrors, he knew his own face when he saw it.

The mouth in his face opened. His own voice said shakily, "Oh *no!*"

"What's happened?" Caspar said, hoping it was not as he feared. But that hope was almost gone when he found himself speaking in Malcolm's cool, precise voice. He dived round and made for the mirror, and the false Caspar opposite him did the same. They fought and jostled to get in front of it. Like that, shoving and pushing with arms and legs rather shorter and weaker than he was used to, Caspar managed to look into his own eyes. Sure enough, they were Malcolm's cool gray ones. Above them was Malcolm's smooth hair; below, Malcolm's nose and precise mouth. And beside him, Malcolm was staring out of Caspar's brown eyes at Caspar's shaggy black hair, with an expression of acute horror on Caspar's face.

"What's the antidote?" Caspar demanded in Malcolm's voice.

"I don't know," Malcolm said helplessly in Caspar's.

"Well, let's find out!" Caspar said desperately.

Sally's voice bawled from downstairs. "Malcolm! Caspar! If you don't come down this minute, you'll both be late for school!"

"What shall we do?" said Malcolm.

"We'll have to go down," said Caspar. "We only had a lick. It might wear off."

"Hurry up!" boomed the Ogre's voice. After that, neither of them dared linger. Caspar dived across the landing for his schoolbag, Malcolm snatched up his and, one behind the other, they pounded downstairs to the kitchen.

Douglas was just getting up to leave. "You've got the wrong bag," he said to Caspar, thinking he was Malcolm.

"So's Caspar," said Gwinny.

"Are you two all right?" asked Sally. "You both look white as ghosts. You haven't time for cereal. Here's your eggs."

The thought of eggs—or indeed anything else—after that powder made both of them feel sick. "I don't think I want an egg," Malcolm said faintly.

The Ogre took his head out of the newspaper and glared at him. "Your mother's cooked it, so you'll eat it," he said. "And take that look off your face, boy."

Caspar looked at his own egg with loathing and silent resentment. The Ogre always picked on him, not Malcolm. And, even if this time it was really Malcolm he was picking on, it was still not fair. "I don't want my egg, either," he said.

"You heard what I said to Caspar," said the Ogre, and hid

his head in the newspaper again.

Reluctantly, they both opened their eggs and toyed with the contents. Caspar wondered what had possessed the lunatic who first thought of eggs as food.

"You'd better go, Johnny. And you, Gwinny," said Sally. "There's no need for you to be late as well."

Johnny, as he got up to go, stopped behind Malcolm's chair. Taking him for Caspar, he whispered, "Was it true, or not?" Caspar saw an expression of complete bewilderment spread over his own face. Its eyes glanced at him for help. He gave it a very small nod.

"True," Malcolm said in a firm whisper. Johnny looked satisfied.

"Get on with your breakfast, Caspar," said Sally.

Johnny and Gwinny left. The real Caspar and the false picked at their eggs again. Each was hoping that the powder would wear off before they were forced to go to school, for it was quite clear that they could not go as they were. And each was determined never, ever to tell a soul what had happened. The mere idea of the way Johnny would laugh made Caspar squirm. Probably Douglas would laugh even louder—at any rate Caspar could tell that Malcolm felt exactly as he did about it. His own face was extraordinarily easy to read. Malcolm's thoughts flitted over it almost as clearly as if he had spoken them. It was the strangest part of the whole horrible experience. He had never been able to tell what Malcolm was thinking before. He wondered if Malcolm found his own face as easy to understand.

Meanwhile they dillied. They dallied. Since the powder showed no sign of wearing off, both clutched their heads and tried to look ill. Both left their eggs half-eaten.

"I've had enough of this," said the Ogre. "My car is going to be at the front of the house in one minute. If I have to fetch you out to it, neither of you is going to enjoy sitting in it."

They saw there was no help for it and went to get their coats. Each naturally took his own without thinking, and then had to change, because Malcolm's coat would not fit Caspar's body. And they had to change schoolbags as well.

"If we can't get out of it," Malcolm whispered, "we'll have to change classes, too, I suppose. Do you agree? I can't tell a thing you're thinking."

This surprised Caspar. He had to think about it for a moment. "You know," he said, "I think your face is bad at showing expressions. *I've* never been able to tell what you're thinking, either."

"Really?" said Malcolm, in considerable astonishment. "But I always know what I—"

Sally came out of the kitchen in her coat. "Are you two still here?" she exclaimed. "Get out to the car at once."

By the time they came out of the front door, the Ogre's thumb was on the horn button and the Ogre's face like thunder. "Sally and I," he said, "are going to be late for work. I've a good mind to take the day off and help your headmaster cane you."

He drove them to the school and dropped them at the main gate. Since one of the masters was just going in as they arrived, Caspar and Malcolm were helpless. All they could do was pelt toward the lines of people going into assembly and remember to join the class that matched their bodies.

Chapter 7

ong before the morning was over, Caspar had given up dreading that he was going to turn suddenly into himself again in front of the whole class. Instead, he gave himself up to despair, muddle, and boredom. He had simply no idea which group Malcolm was in for any subject. By the time he discovered that it was usually the most advanced, it was time for French, and Malcolm turned out to be bad at French. Caspar arrived late and out of breath. Mr. Martin said, "Ah, the Absent-Minded Professor is with us, I see." This relieved Caspar's mind a little, because it looked as if Malcolm was always in a muddle—although he did not like the way the rest of the group laughed. But it did not make up for having the same lesson, word for word, that he had had himself exactly a year before. Nor was it any comfort to know that the French test Malcolm was doing in his place at that moment was certainly going to get zero out of ten—or worse, if that was possible.

The first thing he did at break was to hunt for his own body among all the other people. He found himself extraordinarily hard to recognize at a distance. Malcolm evidently had the same trouble. It was halfway through break before they succeeded in meeting. Caspar found his own face looking quite haggard.

"This is awful!" Malcolm said. "I can't understand a word. You had a French test and I got you zero, I'm afraid."

"I was going to, anyway," said Caspar. "Don't worry. It's an emergency, after all. Let's say we're ill and get sent home."

"But they take your temperature," said Malcolm. "And I bet we're both normal."

"Normal!" said Caspar. "Let's just go home, then."

"And someone finds out and tells Father?" said Malcolm. "You go, if you want."

"I don't want," said Caspar.

"I tell you what," said Malcolm, "suppose we skip lunch and belt round to that toy shop and ask him for the antidote. Because I don't think we're going to change without one, do you?"

"No," agreed Caspar. "But I can't *bear* missing lunch. After no breakfast I'm starving already. What lunch are you?"

"Second."

"And you go to first as me," said Caspar. "That gives us half an hour. Meet you outside the canteen. And tell me which group you're in for math."

"Hunter's," said Malcolm. "And who are your friends?"

Caspar was reciting the names of his friends, and Malcolm was nodding and saying he was glad, he had worked most of them out right, then, when Johnny came up and took hold of Malcolm by the elbow.

"Oh, do come on, Caspar," he said. "We're waiting."

Malcolm, with an apologetic look at Caspar, went off with Johnny. Caspar, before he remembered, had a moment of purest seething fury that they should march off and leave him like that. Then he realized that this was exactly what he and

Johnny usually did do. For the rest of break, he wandered moodily and dismally round by himself, working out the implications of this, and arguing against his conscience that he was *not* mean to Malcolm. Oh no, Malcolm went out of his way to insult them both, anyway. But, argue as he might, the fact remained that Malcolm was supposed to be part of their family now, and neither he nor Johnny had made the slightest attempt to look after him at school.

"But think how he jeers," Caspar told his conscience. And his conscience smartly returned that one by reminding him that Malcolm's face was not good at showing feelings, and asking Caspar what he would do himself if he were too proud to beg someone to be friends.

At this point, it occurred to Caspar that no friends had come up to him at all, during lessons or during break, and that he had been wandering round entirely and gloomily alone— as he remembered seeing Malcolm doing. And he felt more wretched than ever.

Then came an appallingly boring math lesson. After that, Caspar discovered that Malcolm's situation was worse than he had realized. The last session before lunch was craft. Everyone gathered at tables with paint, wood, paper, and clay, and everything got much more free and easy. Malcolm was making a boat. It was such a good boat, too, that Caspar was afraid to spoil it by doing anything to it, so he had to pretend. While he was busy pretending, a group of girls came up and tried to drip paint on the boat.

Caspar snatched it away to safety. "You do that again and see what you get!"

The girls burst out laughing and mimicked what he said.

Caspar found Malcolm's cheeks hot. For Malcolm's stiff face seemed incapable of talking in anything but a precise, posh way, and Caspar was well aware that he had mimicked Malcolm himself as often as he could.

Realizing this made him unobservant for a moment. He did not see one of the girls creeping round the other side of him until it was too late. He pounced round, but she had already snatched the boat away. With screams of laughter, the girls passed it to the boys, and the boys tossed it from one to another, inviting Caspar to come and get it. It was a fragile as well as a beautiful boat. Caspar was in agonies in case they broke it. He felt he had no option but to defend Malcolm's property, and he started after it.

Immediately, his way was barred by a peculiarly unpleasant boy called Dale Curtis, grinning nastily. "And where do you think you're off to?" he said.

Caspar, with his eye anxiously on Malcolm's boat—which someone was now balancing on a ruler—was forced to a standstill. He never had liked Dale Curtis—in fact, now he came to think of it, 3H were an awful lot of kids altogether, and it was hard on Malcolm having to be in with them—but Dale Curtis, being a year younger, had never bothered him before. Now, half a head shorter than he was used to, and with a feeling that his shorter arms were not very strong ones, Caspar found Dale Curtis quite a different proposition.

"You're not supposed to run about in craft," said Dale, who had been doing nothing else himself since the lesson started. "Get back to your table like a good little boy."

Caspar saw that he had no choice but to fight Malcolm's battle for him. It made it rather easier that it was his own for the moment. "Get out of my way," he said.

Dale drew breath to mimic him, and gave Caspar his chance. He weighed in with a trick that he and Johnny thought was probably judo. It was not so effective as usual, because Malcolm's arms were really so weak, but it served to tip Dale off balance. And while he swayed, Caspar hit him as hard as he could. The force of the punch almost broke Malcolm's arm— but Caspar knew it had to be hard to do any good. Dale fell over a chair, red-faced and swearing, and Caspar was able to walk over to the boy balancing the boat on the ruler. The boy handed him the boat without a word. Caspar took it, trying not to show that his hand had been numbed by Dale's teeth. Malcolm's poker face helped considerably there.

Then, of course, Mrs. Tremlett noticed something was going on and hurried over. "What's the matter with Dale?"

Half a dozen boys drew breath to say Malcolm McIntyre had hit him. Caspar glared round them, forcing as much threat into Malcolm's face as Malcolm's face would hold. It did the trick. Nobody spoke.

"Dale?" said Mrs. Tremlett.

"I fell over," Dale said, glowering at Caspar in a way that suggested further trouble coming.

None, however, came just then, though one of the girls— the 3H girls seemed to Caspar a really terrible lot—said, "I'm going to tell Mr. Hunter what you did to Dale."

"Right. I'll make sure I find you after that," said Caspar.

They left him alone then. He had a lonely kind of peace through the rest of craft, and through lunch. Malcolm was waiting for him outside the canteen. They set off at once to trot the distance into town.

"I had to hit Dale Curtis," Caspar panted after a while, "or they'd have broken your boat."

Malcolm said nothing. But Caspar could tell from his own readable face that Malcolm was ashamed Caspar had found out the way the class treated him.

"I think they're a horrible crowd," Caspar said.

"Yours are nicer," Malcolm panted curtly.

"Specially the girls," puffed Caspar. Malcolm said nothing. "And Dale's going to be after you," Caspar continued. "I'll teach you some of our judo, if you like."

"I can manage," Malcolm panted.

"Then hit him hard. Ever so hard," Caspar advised. After that he was too breathless to go on.

They trotted hard, until, with heaving chests, they came into a little old yard-place, almost beside the Ogre's office-block and quite dwarfed underneath it. Caspar had never seen the place before, but Malcolm evidently knew it, for he made straight for a dark little shop there. The name over the window was *Magicraft Ltd.* and in the window were a variety of toys, including a chemistry set like the ones the Ogre had bought. It looked a good shop.

Malcolm pushed open the door. An old-fashioned bell tinged, and their laboring lungs drew in strange, spicy smells. An old man in crescent-moon-shaped spectacles pottered out from the dark space behind a scarred and aged counter, and pushed his glasses up to stare at them. They stood, thoroughly out of breath and rather shy, staring back at him and at the string bags full of footballs, the miniature golf clubs, the tool-sets, and the dolls that dangled above the counter and framed the old man.

"Speak up, speak up," said the old man. "Early closing today. I close in five minutes."

"Well," said Caspar, "you know those chemistry sets—"

The old man nodded, and they saw he had a gold-embroidered skullcap on his head. "I do indeed. Those are one of our best lines. But all our goods give satisfaction or money back, you know. I hope you haven't come to complain."

"No, not really," said Malcolm. "It's that powder called *Misc. Pulv.*—"

"Failed to give results?" said the old man, with his eyebrows mounting nearly to his skullcap. He looked with interest from one to the other and—though, maybe, it was simply that his eyebrows being raised so high made his face seem so droll— he appeared to be highly but secretly amused by what he saw. "Now that surprises me," he said.

They were fairly sure the old man knew just what had happened. That, in a way, was a relief, although it did not seem fair to them that he should laugh at their troubles. Both opened their mouths to explain further, but, as they did so, the bell tinged behind them. Someone else came into the shop. Caspar and Malcolm looked at one another. It was going to be fairly embarrassing to explain in front of another customer. Nevertheless, Malcolm said, "Yes, it gave results. But—"

The old man shifted his half-moon glasses and looked beyond him. "Good day to you, my dear sir."

To their consternation, the Ogre's voice replied, "Good day to you." Caspar's brown eyes met Malcolm's gray ones, and they both wondered whether to turn and run. "Hello, you two," said the Ogre genially. "Preparing to be late this afternoon as well, are you?"

"I think we'd better go now," said Caspar, in Malcolm's primmest manner.

"I'll drive you back," said the Ogre. "Fascinating place, this, isn't it? What's your latest line?" he asked the old man.

"I've some very nice footballs," said the old man, and he turned a moon-spectacled eye on Caspar and Malcolm. He might have been calculating whether footballs would please them, but they both thought the look was distinctly malicious. "Just wait while I fetch them down, sir."

The two boys stood helpless while the old man brought a boathook and hooked down a string bag of bright pink footballs, and the Ogre, hands in pockets and pipe in mouth, admired them. The Ogre was the last person they wanted to know about *Misc. Pulv.* Caspar and Malcolm were perfectly sure that the old man knew it and that he was not going to tell them the antidote if he could help it. He chattered to the Ogre about how good these footballs were and how poor most footballs were these days, and the Ogre agreed that footballs were not what they were in his young days, until Caspar and Malcolm grew desperate. One after another, they bobbed forward and tried to whisper to the old man.

"Ah, you can see they're keen," said the old man gleefully to the Ogre. "Boys always know a good football when they see one."

"I'll take two," said the Ogre.

"What's the antidote?" Caspar managed to whisper.

"Eh?" said the old man. "That'll be eighty pence, sir, and cheap at the price, if I may say so. And can I trouble you to leave now, as I'm closing? My early day, you know."

"Of course," said the Ogre. "Come along, you two."

Caspar lingered. Malcolm hung back. "Just a moment," Malcolm said.

"Early closing," said the old man firmly.

"Come along," said the Ogre, more firmly still.

Despite all their efforts to loiter, in two seconds they were outside the door of the shop, each clutching a pink football he did not want. A key clicked in the door of the shop. A blind came down behind the glass, with the word CLOSED painted on it. That was that. As the Ogre led the way to the car park, Malcolm looked at Caspar despairingly.

"Early closing means we've got to stay like this until lunchtime tomorrow," he said.

"I *know*," said Caspar. "What did you have to make me taste that stuff for?"

"It was your fault. You called me a liar. Watch out," said Malcolm. "Don't forget I'm bigger than you now."

"As if I cared!" said Caspar.

The Ogre turned round, looking his most sinister. "Is something troubling you?" he inquired. "Nothing I can't settle by crashing your heads together, I hope? And how about a word of thanks for the footballs?"

"Oh—thank you," they said, and miserably followed him to the car. When he had dropped them at the school, they stood just inside the gate wondering what on earth to do with the footballs. They were so very pink.

"I suppose he meant to be kind," Malcolm said drearily. "Would Gwinny like them?"

Caspar thought he had never hated the Ogre more. "No, she wouldn't. She hates pink. Let's try leaving them in the cloakroom. Someone's bound to steal them. What are we going to *do*?"

"Stay this way till tomorrow, I suppose," Malcolm said, sighing heavily. "There's the bell. Come on."

They trudged off to endure the afternoon. Caspar had hoped that it would not be too bad, since Malcolm's year had football. But Malcolm played goal. Caspar, who liked to be up front somewhere, had never kept goal in his life, and he let in almost every shot.

"I thought that was one thing you were good at!" someone said to him disgustedly afterward.

"Yes," Caspar snapped, thoroughly weary and cross. "But I broke my arm on Dale Curtis this morning." And he marched away to the cloakroom, longing to get home. To his annoyance, the boy followed him, apologizing. Caspar was just about to get rid of him, when it came to him that Malcolm could do with a friend—or he could, if he was going to have to be Malcolm for the rest of his life. So they talked about how horrible Dale Curtis was all the way to the cloakrooms. The two pink footballs were still there. Nobody had even wanted to steal them. Malcolm was there too, looking at them morbidly.

"What on earth are those?" said the boy.

"Ogre's eyeballs," said Caspar. Malcolm gave a scream of insane laughter.

"Not off his rocker, is he?" asked the boy.

"No, but he's not quite himself today," said Caspar.

He and Malcolm walked home together, nursing the footballs and mournfully considering all the possible troubles and misunderstandings waiting for them at home.

"But don't tell anyone," Malcolm insisted.

"Not a darned soul," Caspar agreed.

"Caspar's become friends with Malcolm," Johnny reported to Gwinny. "Would you believe that? They've both got pink footballs to prove it."

"Why?" said Gwinny. "Can I borrow a toffee-bar?"

"Only if you get out. I've got some experiments to do," said Johnny. "If you ask me, it's sinister. Caspar was awfully strange at school, too."

Caspar was fairly sure Johnny was suspicious, but there was nothing he could do about it. He did his best to behave like Malcolm. He went up to the tidy room and put the pink football very neatly away in the glass cupboard, which was a thing he was sure Malcolm would have done. But as soon as Douglas came in, he realized how little he really knew about Malcolm's habits, and had to hurry away downstairs before Douglas started asking awkward questions. There he found Malcolm had solved his share of the difficulties. Caspar came into the kitchen, and there was Malcolm helping Sally get supper and chattering away to her gaily. Sally, thinking he was Caspar, was talking happily back.

Caspar stood in the doorway, overwhelmed with jealous rage and suspicion. He knew he was being unreasonable. He knew Sally was supposed to be Malcolm's mother too now. But he could not get over the feeling that this was a really underhand trick. And the worst of it was that Malcolm looked so cheerful that Caspar had a horrible notion that, if they were to find the antidote, Malcolm was enjoying himself so much as Caspar that he might choose to stay that way. Then what would become of him? As soon as he could, he caught Malcolm in the dining room.

"You mean sneak! What do you mean by sucking up to my mother like that?"

"I wasn't!" Malcolm said indignantly. "I was keeping out of Johnny's way. And it's nice talking to Sally. I like her."

"But not when she thinks you're me. Why don't you talk to her that way when you're yourself, if you like her that much?" said Caspar, grinding Malcolm's teeth.

"Because it's not so easy. Because Douglas— Anyway, you don't think I *like* being you, do you?" said Malcolm.

"No, but I do," Caspar said, and stormed off to the Ogre's study, feeling both angry and relieved.

But the real trouble came after supper, when the Ogre demanded peace and quiet and everyone retreated upstairs. Then Caspar was forced to go into the same room as Douglas and do his best to behave like Malcolm in front of the person who probably knew Malcolm best of all. He was very nervous. Douglas sat down at the table by the window and spread out a great many books. Caspar, hoping this was the right thing to do, sat down opposite him and opened Malcolm's schoolbag. As Malcolm, he had been given French and math. He began to do them, in Malcolm's small neat writing, but with his own brain, which found them easy and boring. He had plenty of space to think in, and he could not help thinking that to work this way—instead of sprawling on an untidy bed as he usually did—was very grown up and comfortable. He began to feel a little smug, and to wonder if Malcolm was getting on so well.

"Hey, Malcolm," Douglas said suddenly. "Who was inside-right for Sheffield Wednesday in 1948?"

Caspar had never dreamed Malcolm knew this sort of thing. He had no idea. He could no more tell Douglas than if

Douglas had asked him the Chinese for scrambled eggs. "I don't know," he said. "I've forgotten."

"Come off it," said Douglas. "You knew yesterday."

"But since then I've had a—had a lapse of memory," Caspar invented desperately. "I think it may be a kind of stroke."

"Kids don't have strokes," Douglas said. He looked up and, for the first time, surveyed the quaking Caspar narrowly. "Are you playing secretive again?" he said. "I thought I'd cured you of that."

"No. Oh no," said Caspar. "It's ambrosia, or something. There's a name for it."

"Amnesia," said Douglas. He looked at Caspar very hard. "What have you been up to? Have you done something stupid with that chemistry set again?"

"I— No— Well, only in a sort of way," said Caspar. Douglas looking very menacing, began to rise from his chair. Caspar pushed his own chair back and braced his legs ready. "No, I didn't. Nothing," he said.

"*I told you not to do it when I wasn't there!*" Douglas roared. His chair fell over behind him and he dived round the table at Caspar. Caspar knocked his own chair over getting out of the way. And something in the way he dodged, or looked, must have been wrong. Douglas stopped, put his eyebrows down, and examined him again. "What's going on here?" he said. "I'll get it out of you if I have to take you apart!" Then he dived for Caspar again.

Caspar dodged him and fled him round the room. But when someone as large as Douglas is determined to catch someone Malcolm's size, he does it. Douglas caught Caspar just by the door. He shook him with great vigor.

"Come on, own up," he said. "Which of them are you? What have you done with Malcolm?"

"I'm Caspar," Caspar admitted, as clearly as his wildly nodding head would let him. "He's me. And it was his fault, too."

"*You—!*" Douglas started to roar.

The door opened and Sally said, "*Douglas!* What on earth are you doing to poor Malcolm?"

Douglas, still keeping tight hold of Caspar's arm, became very correct and distant. "I'm not doing anything to Malcolm," he said, truly enough.

"Then why are you crashing and roaring and shaking him like that?" Sally said. "You really must be careful. He's a lot smaller than you are."

"I know that," Douglas agreed politely. "I haven't hurt him."

"*Yet,*" said Sally. "Come off it, Douglas. You looked ready to kill him when I came in."

"But I haven't," said Douglas.

"Malcolm," Sally said to Caspar, "are you really all right?"

Caspar would have loved to say *No! Save me!* But he did not dare, with Douglas gripping his arm. "I'm all right," he said, in Malcolm's prim little voice.

Sally looked from one to the other. "Oh, why are you two so restrained and uptight all the time?" she said despairingly. "I sometimes think it's no good trying to get to know you. You simply won't make any advances, will you?"

Caspar found this frankness of Sally's embarrassing enough. Douglas, knowing he had hold of Caspar, not Malcolm, plainly found it even worse. His face went scarlet.

"Perhaps it's our Scottish ancestry," he suggested uneasily.

"I think it's just my voice, with me," Caspar claimed urgently, hoping his mother would take the hint and see he needed help.

Sally did not understand, though she grasped the urgency. "I've discovered that, Malcolm," she said kindly, and turned to go. Caspar despaired. But Sally was plainly thinking the situation over. She halted at the door and turned back. "Malcolm," she said, "come downstairs and talk to me while I do the ironing. I could do with some company."

Caspar looked up at Douglas. Most grudgingly, Douglas let go of his arm, and gave him a grim look behind Sally's back. Caspar could not resist smiling with triumph as he followed Sally downstairs.

Chapter 8

Caspar spent the next hour or so sitting on the kitchen table attempting to fold shirts and talking to Sally, while the radio softly played music behind him. It was very comfortable. Caspar chattered away, and found that it made no difference that he was supposed to be Malcolm. His mother talked to him in just the same way. He thought he had better tell Malcolm.

At length, when the last shirt was folded and the ironing board put away, Sally said, "Well, I suppose you'd better get up to bed. I've enjoyed this talk." Caspar looked at her and found it must be true. She looked far less tired and harrowed than usual. So he said good night and went softly upstairs.

He had decided what to do. His plan was to creep up to Gwinny's room and explain to her. Since he had already confessed to Douglas, that seemed fair—and Gwinny was not so likely to laugh as Johnny. The real difficulty was getting past the landing below without Douglas hearing. Never had Caspar moved so quietly. He stole across the landing like a thief, and was rather glad that he had Malcolm's lighter feet to do it on. There was no sound from Douglas's room, no sign that he had heard. Heartily relieved, Caspar reached the next stairway and put on speed for Gwinny's room and safety.

Douglas was waiting on the turn of these stairs. He grabbed Caspar so hard and unexpectedly that Caspar let out a high, mouse-like squeak. He struggled madly, but Douglas was far too strong for him.

"I thought this was what you'd do!" Douglas said triumphantly. "Come on down. And don't dare make a noise."

He dragged the helpless Caspar back downstairs to the landing. Then he hauled him across, not to his own room, but to Caspar's and Johnny's, and threw open its door without knocking. He revealed Malcolm, as Caspar, standing by the opposite wall with a neat pile of comics in his arms, looking exasperated; Johnny kneeling by the chemistry set surrounded by tubes and bottles, looking indignant; and Gwinny sitting on Caspar's bed, looking distressed and puzzled.

Their heads all whipped round as Douglas burst in dragging what appeared to be Malcolm. An expression of alarm came into the real Malcolm's face at the sight of them. But he tried hard to look simply exasperated. "Did you knock?" he said, in a very fair imitation of Caspar's usual manner.

"All right, Malcolm. Come on out of it," said Douglas.

Malcolm looked at Caspar, and Caspar, as far as Malcolm's stiff face would let him, tried to show that the game was up. Malcolm understood. He looked more alarmed than ever, and backed against the wall. "You've gone mad," he said.

"Stark, raving bonkers," Johnny agreed loudly. "Don't you know your own brother when you see him?"

"Yes," said Douglas. "Even when he looks like Caspar. Come on, Malcolm. I rumbled him an hour ago."

"I don't understand," said Malcolm firmly. Caspar knew it

must be very hard for him to admit what had happened in front of Johnny and Gwinny.

"Nor do I understand," Johnny said aggressively.

"We changed places, you nit," said Caspar. "It was a sort of accident. And it was your fault really, sending me to talk to him."

Johnny stared from one to the other with his mouth open. To Caspar's relief, he showed no inclination to laugh—he was far too surprised. Gwinny bounced up from Caspar's bed. "Oh, you *are* Caspar!" she said. "I can tell it's you talking. I couldn't think what had happened, especially when you started tidying up."

"If you want any proof, that's it," said Douglas. "Did any of you ever see Caspar tidy up? Come on, Malcolm."

"No," said Malcolm.

"Right," said Douglas, and, towing Caspar, he plunged across the room, ploughing through comics and scattering construction kits. Malcolm made a very feeble effort to dodge, and Caspar saw that this was where he had gone wrong. Malcolm must have learned long ago that when Douglas was determined to get him, get him he would. He got him very easily this time, by the shirt collar. "Right," he said. "Now you're coming back to our room to find the antidote." Pushing the two of them in front of him, as if they were the front part of a bulldozer, he ploughed them back across the room.

"Hey! Watch it!" Johnny cried indignantly, as the chemistry set leaped aside under their six flying feet. The tubes and bottles rattled together and tipped. Johnny threw himself forward and just saved a mass spill. But one of Douglas's large feet kicked against the bottle Johnny had put down in order to catch the others, and sent it flying into the heap of plastic shapes Johnny was using to support test-tubes. Johnny threw himself after it and picked it up all but empty. "Now look what you've done!" he said. Caspar looked at the bottle anxiously. It seemed to be the one called *Animal Spirits* that Malcolm said was dull. So probably no harm was done.

Douglas thought the same. "One more mess won't be noticed in this pigsty," he called over his shoulder, propelling Caspar and Malcolm to the door.

"It's nearly empty!" said Johnny.

"Too bad," said Douglas.

"Pig yourself!" said Johnny.

"Can I come and watch?" Gwinny called after Douglas.

"No. Go to bed," said Douglas.

Probably Gwinny would have protested. But the Ogre arrived on the landing as Douglas was running Caspar and Malcolm across it.

"Douglas, what *is* going on?" he said.

Douglas stopped in his tracks, but he kept tight hold of the other two. Inside Johnny's and Caspar's room, Gwinny struggled hurriedly under Caspar's bed and tried not to sneeze in the fluff there. Johnny leapt into his own bed with all his clothes on, even his shoes, and pretended to be asleep.

"Nothing," Douglas said uneasily.

"A—a game we're playing," Malcolm added guiltily.

"Called troikas," Caspar supplied inventively.

"In which you harness three elephants to a sledge and gallop hard over the frozen floorboards," agreed the Ogre. "*Stop!*"

"We will when we've got to our room," said Douglas. "That's our base." He put the other two in motion with a push and a tweak, and they all scurried to the room opposite, where Malcolm humbly opened the door for them. The Ogre, having watched them go in, went to the open door of the other room. Gwinny and Johnny lay like ramrods.

"What horrible squalor," remarked the Ogre, and turned off the light and went downstairs. Gwinny scrambled out from under the bed, seized the nearest toffee-bar, and raced up to her room before she started sneezing. Johnny went to sleep as he was.

In the other room, Douglas said, "What was it? Something you ate?"

"Yes," said Caspar.

"*Misc. Pulv.,*" admitted Malcolm.

"You little twits!" said Douglas. "Right. Then we'll take that out, and you'll both have to eat some of everything else in the box until we find the antidote."

Their stomachs heaved a little at the thought. "What if that doesn't work?" asked Malcolm.

"Then you try each one again in combination with one of the others," said Douglas. "And then with two others, and so on. Even if it takes all night."

And that was just what he made them do. An hour later, they had gone all through everything once and were halfway through taking them all again with salt. Malcolm suggested they try salt first. "That's what I put with *Parv. Pulv.* to go small," he explained.

"Then we won't use *Parv. Pulv.* this round," said Douglas.

Caspar supposed he should be thankful. It made one less

chemical to eat. By this time, he was feeling decidedly ill, and he could see Malcolm was too. When they came to *Animal Spirits,* which had a sweet, fizzy taste, it was so horrible with salt that they had to beg for a moment to recover.

Douglas was grudging about it. "I think you deserve to feel ill," he said.

"If you knew what a horrible day we've had!" Malcolm cried out. "And Father giving us pink footballs on top of it!"

"Oh all right," said Douglas. "You can have one minute, or we'll be here all night." There was half a minute of silence, except for the gulps of Malcolm and the gasps of Caspar. Douglas unfeelingly watched the second hand of his watch, until, quite suddenly, he forgot all about it and banged his forehead with his fist instead. "What a nit I am! This is no good. You're bound to have to take *Misc. Pulv.* again, to mix yourselves up the other way!"

"No!" said Caspar.

"I couldn't!" said Malcolm.

"Yes, you can," said Douglas. "If you did it once, you can do it again. I don't want to be stuck with Caspar as a roommate, whatever you want. Hold your hands out."

Such was his ferocity that they both meekly did so. Douglas shoveled them out each a generous spoonful of *Misc. Pulv.* The mere smell of it was almost too much for them.

"Eat it," said Douglas. "Go on. I'll count to ten. One— two—"

On the count of eight they still thought they could not. On the count of nine, they wondered. On the count of ten, their nerve broke. Each lifted the nasty handful to his mouth, sucked some of the powder in, and did their best to swallow.

The whirling sensation that came after the appalling taste was the last straw. Gagging, they each opened their watering eyes and stared at the pale face opposite. They felt too ill even to be glad the stuff had worked.

"Has it worked?" Douglas demanded. They nodded, too far gone to speak. "Then don't be sick in here," said Douglas. "Get to the bathroom."

They bolted for the door, tore it open, hammered downstairs shoulder to shoulder to the bathroom, and flung themselves inside it. But by this time, their heaving stomachs had subsided somewhat.

"I think I'm all right now," Malcolm said.

"So am I. Just about," said Caspar.

And they both began to laugh. Malcolm fell across the washbasin, and Caspar doubled up over the towel rail, and they laughed till their eyes watered again.

"Are you boys drunk or something?" demanded the Ogre on the threshold.

Malcolm looked up and caught Caspar's streaming eye. "Eyeballs!" he gasped. They both fell in a heap on the bathmat, laughing hysterically.

"Get up," said the Ogre irritably. "Get to bed. I want to have a bath."

They staggered up and climbed the stairs, whimpering with mirth. Caspar laughed all the time he was crunching about his room hunting for his pajamas, and he was still laughing a little when he went to sleep.

He did not sleep very soundly. He kept having wild dreams—possibly because of all the chemicals he had eaten—and once or twice he woke up almost completely, with a feeling that somebody was walking about the room. But the moon shining between the curtains showed him that no one was there.

He was woken in the morning by a shout from Johnny. "It's that stuff Douglas spilled. Look what it's gone and done!"

Caspar sat up and found Johnny, very scruffy and irritable from having slept in his clothes, standing up on his bed opposite. "What?" said Caspar.

Johnny went suddenly cautious. "Are you Caspar or Malcolm?"

"Caspar," said Caspar. "Break my heart across your knee," he added, seeing that Johnny was still not sure.

Since this was a private family expression, Johnny was satisfied. "How did you get back?" he asked, with scientific interest.

"Douglas made us eat something of everything in the box."

"He would!" said Johnny. "The flipping bully. And look what else he's done. Down on the floor beside your bed."

Caspar leaned over and looked. He saw an oozing, a shimmering, and a writhing. The heap of colored construction kits was in slow, wriggling motion, heaving and seething, each piece moving separately—almost as if it were alive. As Caspar watched, a bright blue plastic brick left this heap and looped its way slowly over an Indigo Rubber record toward his bed. Then it began to crawl up Caspar's trailing blankets, for all the world like a bright blue caterpillar.

"I think they're alive," said Caspar.

"That's what I thought," said Johnny. "They're all over the place, too."

Johnny was right. Now that Caspar looked, he could see

pieces of plastic crawling slowly in every part of the room. A pink, screw-shaped one was climbing the wall beside Johnny's bed. Several of the red kind with holes in them were clinging to the curtains. Green and purple rods of different lengths were looping across comics, in company with red, black, and yellow bricks. A cluster of the flat, gray bits meant to make an airplane was hanging on the edge of the open cupboard door, quivering, not unlike a swarm of bees. Still barely able to believe it, Caspar reached out and plucked the blue brick off his blankets. It was just a small oblong building block, and it felt like plastic, but it nevertheless rotated itself between his finger and thumb as if it were trying to get loose. And when it found it was caught, it tried to curl up into a ball.

"They're alive all right," said Caspar.

"What are we going to do with them all?" Johnny said helplessly. "*Blast* Douglas!"

"What did it?" asked Caspar. *"Animal Spirits?"*

"Yes," said Johnny.

"Malcolm thought that was dull and didn't do anything," said Caspar. "Fat lot he knew!"

"We mustn't let him know," Johnny said. "We'll have to catch them all and hide them somehow."

So Caspar got up and found the four large biscuit tins that Sally had given them to keep the construction kits in, and they set to work to fill them with squirming pieces of plastic. The heap by Caspar's bed was easy enough to catch and scoop into tins—though pieces would keep writhing themselves over the edge of the tin and flopping to the floor—but the bits wandering over the room were quite another matter. It took them nearly an hour to collect them all. And each time they came back to the tins with a new handful, they had to pick up all the bits that had escaped onto the floor, and cram them back into the tins too.

"They're worse than fishing bait," Johnny said crossly. "They look rather like bait, don't they?" Caspar agreed. Even though the pieces of plastic were all colors of the rainbow, they did, all the same, look remarkably like grubs and larvae. "Find the lids," Johnny said. "They'll never stay in all day if we don't shut them up."

By pulling everything out of the cupboard and raking through the resulting heap with an old golf club, Caspar found three of the lids. The fourth lid was missing. They had to cover the remaining tin with comics and stick them down with tape. Johnny taped the other lids, too, to be on the safe side. There began to be quite a noise of soft writhings and tappings, as the imprisoned construction kits tried to get out. By this time it was late. They heard Gwinny going downstairs, followed by Douglas. Caspar had to hurry to get dressed.

"I think I ought to make holes in the lids," Johnny said, while Caspar was hunting for his shirt. "If they're alive, it's not kind if I don't, is it?"

"Well, don't make the holes too big or they'll get out through them," Caspar said, pulling his shirt out from under the heap of things by the cupboard.

Johnny found a skewer in the same heap and hammered away at the lids, punching holes. "Lucky we've got some *Animal Spirits* left still," he called, above the battering. "I wonder what else it works on. I must try. I'd rather like a table that was alive, wouldn't you? It could follow me about until I wanted to use it."

"Could you train it to keep still while you were writing, though?" Caspar wondered. "And you'd have to get it to sham dead in front of the Ogre, or there'd be trouble."

Johnny, quite enraptured with this idea, finished making holes and hunted for the *Animal Spirits* bottle while Caspar tied his shoes. As their mother called up to them to hurry, he found it. He gave a cry of despair.

"Blast Douglas! Blast the Ogre, too! I had to get into bed when he came upstairs and I forgot to put the stopper in. It's all evaporated!"

"Borrow some of Malcolm's," Caspar suggested as they hurried downstairs.

"Catch him lending anything!" Johnny said crossly. "Oh, *blast!*"

He was still cross when they set off for school, and crosser still at break, when Caspar insisted on finding Malcolm.

"What do you want to find *him* for?" he demanded.

"If you'd been him for a day, you'd know why," Caspar retorted, and went off to search. He found Malcolm at the very moment when Malcolm hit Dale Curtis as hard as he could and made Dale's lip bleed. Dale looked so savage at this, and Malcolm so unexpectedly small, that Caspar made haste to range himself beside Malcolm and give Dale the long, menacing look that gangsters give on television. Dale returned it. But he saw he would have to reckon with Caspar Brent as well as Malcolm McIntyre. He decided to leave Malcolm alone for the moment, and strolled loftily away.

"Come and play football with a tennis ball," Caspar invited Malcolm.

Malcolm gingerly flexed a hand that Caspar guessed was numbed. "You don't have to look after me," he said haughtily.

"I'm not," said Caspar. "I knew you wouldn't play. I only asked you because our goalie's no good."

There was a pause. Then Malcolm said graciously. "I'll keep goal for you if you like." Caspar, rather pleased with his cunning, took him over to the game. Johnny did not say anything, but the expression on his face was not pleasant. And Caspar had a premonition that there was going to be trouble with Johnny—bad trouble—perhaps not now, but sometime soon.

Chapter 9

Gwinny, meanwhile, had a queer experience at her school. She was nature monitor, and it was her job to come in before afternoon school and get things ready. It was one of those fine, warm days that happen in late autumn, and, since it was Friday, Gwinny was looking forward to the weekend. The Ogre was going to be away all Saturday and Sunday at a conference and things would be fun for once. Gwinny sang to herself as she gave out pencils and nature folders.

As she leaned forward over the big table in the center of the classroom to push the folders across it, something climbed out of her pocket and landed with a soft *clump* on the table. Gwinny craned her head round. She stared, frozen and bent over. It was the toffee-bar she had borrowed from Johnny, complete with its white and yellow wrapper. And it was crawling across the table in a slow, deliberate way, as if it knew where it was going.

"No, stop! Come back!" Gwinny said to it. She felt all guilty and responsible. The toffee-bar was alive, and she had no doubt that it was the bottle Douglas spilled that had done it. She put down the folders, a little nervously. She was not exactly frightened. The toffee-bar was only four inches long and flat as a ruler. But, even so, if it was alive, it was not precisely a toffee-bar any longer.

The toffee-bar crawled steadily on until it came to a patch of sunlight in the middle of the table. There, it stopped and stretched and coiled itself this way and that with evident enjoyment.

"Oh, do come back!" Gwinny said to it.

But the toffee-bar took no notice. It stretched several times more, rather harder. Then, quite suddenly, the white and yellow paper split in two along the top of it. The toffee inside wriggled a little, and then it crawled out from the paper, a smooth yellow-brown strip.

"I'll have to catch you," Gwinny said firmly. She reached out, not quite so firmly, and tried to take hold of the toffee-bar. It must have seen her hand coming. Its limber brown body jackknifed and leaped away from her fingers. In a flash, it had jumped off the table, wriggled over the floor, and gone to earth in a shelf of library books.

Gwinny had to leave it there, because the rest of the class was coming in. She hurriedly put the cast-off wrapper in her pocket and gave out the rest of the folders. For the rest of the afternoon she was in agony. The toffee-bar just would not stay quiet. Gwinny could hear it slithering and clumping behind the books in the bookshelf, and so could the rest of the class.

"Has somebody brought a mouse in here?" asked Mrs. Clayton.

Nobody answered, but, to judge from the looks and giggles, everybody thought somebody had. Gwinny felt more and more guilty and ashamed.

When everyone went out for P.E. last period, Gwinny

borrowed Linda Davey's handkerchief, because her own was only a tissue, and stayed behind. As soon as she had collected the folders, she set out, with great determination, to trap the toffee-bar by emptying the bookshelf, book by book. The toffee-bar scuttled away from the open spaces, until she had it penned in a corner, behind three Mary Plain books. Then she took those out all at once and pounced. She got it. It wriggled frantically. Gwinny did not like it, because she hated smooth, warmish, wriggly things. But she managed to wrap it in Linda's handkerchief and knot the corners together so that it could not escape. It seemed strong, and Gwinny rather thought it had grown since it cast its wrapper.

Somehow—she did not know why—she was deeply ashamed of it. After school, she avoided all her usual friends and went home secretly by back ways. The toffee-bar was wriggling so wildly by then that Gwinny had to take the knotted handkerchief out of her pocket and hold it hard by the knots in order not to lose it. And she wondered what on Earth she was going to do with it when she did get it home.

It made her later than usual. She reached the front gate at the same time as Malcolm. "What have you got there?" he asked, looking with interest at the bulging, jerking handkerchief. "A mouse?"

Gwinny felt she knew Malcolm quite well now that she had spent a whole evening thinking he was Caspar. Besides, she was desperate to tell someone who would understand. "No, it's a toffee-bar," she said. "And it's rather awful. It's alive."

"Not really?" said Malcolm, and his face went pink with excitement. "Show me."

"Get ready to catch it, then," said Gwinny. "You wouldn't

believe how nimble it is. It got away like a flash before nature this afternoon." Malcolm nodded and held his hands out ready. Gwinny began unknotting the handkerchief. But the toffee-bar was too lithe for either of them. It was out, and slithering down Gwinny's arm, before Malcolm could move. It dodged as he grabbed it, leaped from the hem of Gwinny's coat to the ground, and made off like a yellow-brown streak into the bottom of the hedge. "Oh, bother!" said Gwinny.

Malcolm gave a roar of delighted laughter. "And it really was toffee?" he said. "How splendid! Was it that bottle Douglas kicked over?"

"I think it must have been," said Gwinny.

"How marvelous!" said Malcolm. "Gwinny, I'll give you a big reward for this. Wait and see." And, with a whoop of excitement, he went dashing into the house and pounding up the stairs as heavily as ever Johnny did.

Gwinny followed him. She found the Ogre in the hall, balefully watching Malcolm's flying heels disappearing round the corner. "The habits of your family must be catching," he said to Gwinny. "That *was* Malcolm, wasn't it?"

"Yes," said Gwinny. "He's excited about something."

"Evidently," said the Ogre sourly.

"He's not doing any harm," said Gwinny. "He needed to run about a bit. He's much too old-fashioned usually."

"Old-fashioned?" said the Ogre. "It's odd you should say that. I've always thought you were the old-fashioned one."

"Oh, not me," Gwinny said. "I'm modern. In fact," she said, thinking of the toffee-bar, "I may be quite new-fangled. I've just made a really up-to-date invention."

The Ogre laughed. "Then you'd better take out a patent,"

he said, as he went into the sitting room, "before somebody else steals your invention."

Gwinny went upstairs rather thoughtfully. For the invention, though it had been Douglas who kicked the bottle, might be said to be Johnny's, and she had a feeling Johnny would be furious to know she had told Malcolm. She went past the door of Johnny's and Caspar's room and straight on up to her own.

Beyond that door, Caspar and Johnny were staring fascinated at the six or seven toffee-bars curled up on comics and basking in the afternoon sun. They had all cast their wrappers, and these lay littered about, most of them near the space where the construction kits had been. Johnny set off to catch one of them. Immediately, another toffee-bar darted out from under a comic beside his foot and flashed away toward the cupboard. The basking bars, aroused by the movement, uncurled and shot off, also. In a second, there was not a sign of them, except for a faint rustling here and there.

"Just like lizards," Johnny said, more fascinated still.

Caspar was looking at the cast-off wrappers. "There's an awful lot of these," he said. "Twice as many as we saw."

"Some of them may be off ones we ate," said Johnny.

"How many did we have?" said Caspar.

"No idea," said Johnny.

"Then we'd better count these wrappers," said Caspar. "And find another box to put the toffee-bars in when we do catch them. They're going to get all over the house if we don't look out."

"I'll go down and look for a box," said Johnny. But, before he went, he untaped the lid of one of the biscuit tins and had a look to see how the construction kits were getting on. They seemed to be writhing and heaving much as before, and the inevitable one or two came over the edge and had to be put back. "Oughtn't we to feed them?" he said. "If they are alive."

"Bring some biscuits when you get the box," said Caspar. "The toffee-bars may be hungry, too."

So Johnny rammed the lid back on and went down to the kitchen, while Caspar collected all the toffee-wrappers he could find and made a careful count. It came to nineteen. The thought of catching nineteen nimble toffee-bars was a little daunting. He had only succeeded in catching one by the time Johnny came back with a large cardboard box and a packet of Small Rich Tea Biscuits, and the only reason he caught that one was that Johnny had bitten a piece off it the evening before. It was much slower than the others in consequence, and went with a sort of limp.

"Oh, the poor thing!" Johnny said, when Caspar showed him. "I'll never eat another toffee-bar again!" He put it tenderly in the cardboard box and made it comfortable with some comics and a Small Rich Tea Biscuit. It did not want to stay. Crippled as it was, it kept trying to get out, until Caspar thought of putting the box against the radiator. The lame bar seemed to like that. It curled up peacefully and began to look a little sticky.

Then they tried to catch the eighteen others. After half an hour of tearing around and desperate pouncing, they had caught exactly one each, and both the Ogre and Douglas were roaring for silence. The only thing for it seemed to be to clear the floor.

So, for the first time in their lives, they put everything in the cupboard or on the bookshelves, and piled the other things on the windowsill. And very hard work it was, too. But they had their reward. It was an easy matter then to hunt the flying toffee-bars as they shot along the sides of the room, and almost as easy to catch the ones that retreated under the beds.

"Well, at least we know nothing else came alive now," Caspar said, dusty and triumphant, carrying a whipping hand-ful of toffee-bars over to the radiator and counting them as he dropped them into the box. "Nineteen. That's all of them at last."

The warmth of the radiator pleased their captives. They curled up drowsily among the comics, and Johnny gave them some biscuits. But the biscuits were untouched after supper, and the construction kits had not eaten theirs, either. Johnny became worried. He was leaning over the cardboard box trying to tempt at least the lame bar to eat, when Sally came in.

"What a wonderfully tidy room!" she said. "What have you got in that box?"

"It's my comic-store," said Johnny, deftly pulling a couple of comics over the captives.

"What system!" said Sally, laughing. "Have either of you seen Jack's best pipe? He wants it to go away with." They had not. "I'd better ask Gwinny," said Sally.

When she had gone, Johnny fetched some lettuce, but neither the construction kits nor the toffee-bars seemed to care for lettuce, either. So, on Caspar's advice, Johnny gave the problem up for the moment and started to learn the poem he should have learned last week. Caspar began on his homework.

They were interrupted by a sharp scuttering noise. They

looked up, and then at one another, mystified. The scuttering came again. Johnny pointed. Out from under Caspar's bed, into the middle of the empty floor, came the strangest creature yet. It was dark brown, and moved in a quick, lively way that put them in mind of a miniature squirrel or chipmunk. Yet its small chunky body did not seem to have a recognizable head. It had a long stiff tail that it held high behind it as it ran and that it seemed to use for balance. And it seemed to have a bold and inquiring disposition, for it stopped to sniff with interest at Caspar's foot, which was hanging down from his bed, and its tail quivered as it sniffed.

It took them nearly a minute to recognize the Ogre's pipe, which Gwinny had dropped the night the flying-mixture splashed on her.

"Who was it said nothing else had come alive?" said Johnny.

Caspar could not help laughing. "Let's give it him to go away with," he said, and he got off his bed to catch it. The pipe at once dropped on its side and shammed dead.

"You've frightened it!" said Johnny. "And don't you dare give it to the Ogre. He'd try to light it."

Caspar realized this would be cruel. He got gently back on his bed again, and they waited to see what the pipe would do. It lay for a while. But when neither of them moved, it got up on its bowl again with a powerful whisk of its stem and began scuttering about the carpet, exploring. It seemed very interested in the biscuit tins. For some time it ran round and round on all fours. Then, with a mighty hop, it managed to jump on top of one. There, it scrabbled round the holes Johnny had made and seemed to become increasingly desperate. It uttered a tiny agitated squeak or so.

"I think it wants it open," said Johnny. "Shall I open one?"

"Yes," said Caspar. "Let's see what it does then."

Johnny stole heavily over to the tins. The pipe took fright and hid from him, by jumping into the gap between two tins. But when Johnny had taken off a lid and retreated, it came boldly out and hopped up onto the edge of the open tin. They watched it bend forward over the writhing plastics, with its tail cocked for balance and quivering. Its bowl moved, and they both distinctly heard a golloping.

"It's eating them!" Johnny exclaimed.

Having fed largely and, incidentally, solved two of their problems at one go, the pipe decided they were friendly and went roaming boldly about the room. Caspar could not resist fetching Gwinny to see it. Gwinny was enthralled. The Ogre's pipe so enchanted her that her lack of surprise and interest in the toffee-bars passed unnoticed—to her great relief.

"Show Mummy," she said. "She'll love it."

But Johnny refused, on the grounds that Sally could not be trusted not to tell the Ogre. At this, Gwinny became rather thoughtful and went away as soon as she could.

The Ogre left Saturday morning. There was a wonderful feeling of freedom without him, though this was a little spoiled for Caspar by Johnny worrying about what toffee-bars ate. To make up for starving them, Johnny turned the cardboard box on its side and let the toffee-bars have the freedom of the room. He put them down a saucer of water. The pipe, when it wanted a drink, drove the toffee-bars off with a vicious curving rush that sent them scattering all over the room, but, otherwise, it took no notice of them.

All the same, the toffee-bars had definitely grown. Caspar

could not see what Johnny was worrying about. He played Indigo Rubber full blast and refused to listen to him. Across the landing, Douglas's guitar thrummed. Then Douglas went off on his bicycle and returned with two Indigo Rubber records of his own.

"Thank heaven Jack can't hear this," Sally said, when both record players were going.

"I think it's because he isn't here," Malcolm explained.

"I'm aware of that," Sally said wryly. "And I'm going shopping. Who's coming?"

Gwinny and Malcolm both went, and not only did they help Sally and spend their pocket money, but they had coffee with Sally in a snack bar and enjoyed themselves very much. Gwinny found she was liking Malcolm more and more, and she was rather pleased to see that Sally seemed to like him, too. In fact, she enjoyed herself so much that she began to feel disloyal to Johnny and Caspar.

After lunch, Caspar and Johnny came into their room to find toffee-bars all along the edge of the carpet, nibbling it. They had eaten it quite frayed. Johnny's relief was boundless.

"It's the fluffy part they seem to like," he observed, inspecting the damage. "Can I give them your green sweater?"

"No," said Caspar, who was fond of that green sweater. "But Gwinny's probably got some she's grown out of."

They went up to Gwinny's room to ask. To their surprise, Douglas and Malcolm were just coming down from it. Douglas was carrying a bucket of water—the selfsame bucket with which Johnny had drenched Gwinny and Caspar that first fateful night. Maybe it was the associations of that bucket, or something about Douglas's or Malcolm's manner, but Johnny instantly suspected dirty work of some kind.

"What have you been doing to Gwinny?" he demanded.

"Nothing," said Malcolm.

"Go and ask her if you like," said Douglas.

Johnny and Caspar squeezed past Douglas and hurried up to Gwinny's room. Gwinny was kneeling in the middle of it, and it was evident that she had been crying. But she stoutly denied that Douglas and Malcolm had harmed her in any way.

"They were very kind," she said.

"Then why are you crying?" Johnny asked accusingly.

"About something else," said Gwinny. "I was being silly, and Malcolm made me feel better. I like Malcolm. So there!" She trembled a little after making this awful admission, and she did not dare go on to say that she had always secretly admired Douglas. To her relief, Caspar took it well. Johnny, of course, was utterly disgusted.

"Flipping girls!" he said. "Give me some old sweaters for the toffee-bars and then don't come near me for a month. You stink!"

Gwinny handed over two sweaters, thankful that she had got off so lightly, and the boys took them away downstairs.

"That bucket," said Johnny. "You don't think they were brainwashing her, do you?"

"You don't brainwash people by dipping their heads in a bucket, you nit!" said Caspar. "Besides, her hair wasn't wet."

The toffee-bars fell on the sweaters so hungrily that, by Sunday evening, only the ribbing-parts were left. The toffee-bars, even the lame one, had grown to the size of twelve-inch rulers. Caspar felt a little uneasy about them. He wished they were like the pipe which, in spite of having eaten nearly half a tin of construction kits, had remained exactly the same size.

The room began to smell, rather. By Sunday evening, it was horrible.

"I think it's their droppings," said Johnny. "They're not house-trained, really, you see."

Caspar, knowing the Ogre was due back for supper, hastened downstairs and fetched the vacuum cleaner. The noise frightened the toffee-bars into the back of their box, and the pipe took the long hose of the cleaner for a snake and hid in the cupboard. But at least the smell grew less.

"We'll have that, after you," Douglas said, appearing in the doorway.

"Too lazy to bring it up for yourself, are you?" Johnny said.

"None of your cheek," Douglas replied, and hit him a sharp smack. He took the vacuum cleaner and left Johnny raging.

"You might *say* something, Caspar! He *hit* me! Did you see him?"

"Yes, I saw him," said Caspar. It was hard to know what to do about it. Douglas was technically the eldest, and no one denied the eldest his right to thump younger ones who cheeked him. And Johnny had cheeked Douglas. And Douglas had not hit him hard. And Caspar had no wish to stir Douglas up in case he remembered about the night the Ogre caught him. Besides, he owed it to Douglas that he was not still Malcolm. But, of course, Caspar was really Johnny's elder brother, not Douglas. He could think of only one solution. "It should have been me to hit you, I suppose. I will if you like."

"You're as bad as Gwinny!" said Johnny.

"Well?" said the Ogre at supper. "Did you all have a good weekend?"

"Oh yes!" they said, all five, with what was, everyone saw at once, quite undue enthusiasm.

"I see," said the Ogre sourly.

Johnny swore it was in revenge that the Ogre suddenly appeared in the doorway of their room that evening. Johnny himself was quite legally engaged in puzzling out which of the remaining chemicals belonged to the bottom layer of the chemistry set. The toffee-bars were huddled in the box sleeping off Gwinny's sweaters, and the lids were firmly on the biscuit tins. But Gwinny was there when she should have been in bed. She and Caspar were trying to teach the pipe to do tricks. It would have been hard to say whether Gwinny or the pipe was more frightened when the Ogre came in. The pipe instantly dropped on its side and shammed dead, and Gwinny wished she could, too.

"You've had some sort of revolution here, haven't you?" said the Ogre, seeing the unusually bare room. Then he looked at Gwinny, and Gwinny quailed. But, at that moment, the Ogre saw the pipe. "I've been hunting high and low for that," he said, and, to their horror, he came and picked it up. The pipe shammed dead for all it was worth. "How did it get here?" asked the Ogre.

"It—it came to light after we'd tidied up," said Caspar.

"Did it indeed?" said the Ogre. "Better late than never, I suppose." And, to their further horror, he fetched out his tobacco and began filling the pipe. "I came up to ask you something," he said, packing tobacco into the stiff, terrified creature. "I wondered— Oh, are you here, too? Good."

Douglas and Malcolm were standing in the doorway. "We came to borrow a record," Douglas said, and Caspar thought it sounded remarkably like an excuse.

"Well, I wanted to talk to all of you," the Ogre said, pressing tobacco home. "You know Sally and I are giving this party on Wednesday. A lot of people have been very kind to us, and we wanted to pay them back in style. And we wondered—" Here he struck a match and brought it toward the pipe.

This was too much for the poor pipe. It gave a frantic twist and tried to break loose from the Ogre's hand. The Ogre looked at it rotating and squirming in front of his face as if he thought he had gone mad. Caspar, Johnny, and Gwinny did not know what to do or say. They could only hope that, as the Ogre's back was half-turned toward the door, Malcolm had not noticed what was going on. Douglas could not have seen, because he had fortunately been overcome with a sudden attack of coughing.

The Ogre, plainly thinking he was imagining the whole thing, put the pipe firmly back in his mouth and applied the match to it. The pipe stopped squirming and went stiff again. "We thought that two of you children could act as waiters," the Ogre said, between puffs. "Pass round olives and sandwiches and so on." They hardly heard him. They were all trying to see how the pipe was faring among the clouds of smoke. "Best behavior and suits," said the Ogre, applying another match.

"I'd like that," said Johnny, without the least idea what he was saying. Douglas's cough came on again.

"Would you?" said the Ogre, striking a third match. "Frankly, Johnny, you're the last one I'd choose, left to myself. But Sally said I was to leave it to you."

Johnny found himself forced to defend his mistake. "You can eat an awful lot of crisps and things while you're passing them," he said.

"Precisely," said the Ogre. The pipe was well alight now, and it had given no further sign of life. "Gwinny's too young to stay up, but—"

Gwinny would have made a hearty protest at any other time. Now, all she could think of was that the pipe seemed to be dead. "Oh, I hope it didn't suffer much!" she said. Douglas seemed to have got something badly stuck in his throat. He was coughing fit to burst.

The Ogre looked at Gwinny in some surprise. "So that leaves you boys," he said. "Which of you's going to join Johnny as waiter?"

Douglas looked up, rather wet-eyed, and said firmly, "I've got an awful lot of homework these days."

While Caspar was trying to tear his mind from the terrible end of the pipe and to think of a likely excuse, Malcolm said, "Football. I've got a football match."

"Yes, we've both probably got a football match on Wednesday," said Caspar.

"Very convenient," said the Ogre, puffing blue smoke. The pipe was suddenly making an extraordinary noise. It was plainly not dead yet, and that made them very unhappy. The noise was a kind of rumbling and a rasping. Caspar thought it must be the poor thing's death-rattle, but it went on and on and sounded almost too placid for that.

Gwinny realized what it was. "The pipe!" she said. "It's purring!" It was, almost as loudly as Douglas was coughing. Johnny and Caspar were too relieved for words.

"Not really," said the Ogre. "They make this noise when they need cleaning. Then, since you three so plainly can't decide, I suggest you toss for it."

Douglas recovered. "I want two volunteers: you and you," he said hoarsely. The Ogre looked at him unpleasantly over the purring pipe. "Well, it is a bit like that, isn't it?" said Douglas.

The Ogre, without answering, took out a coin and spun it. "Heads or tails, Caspar?"

Malcolm won the toss, and looked very dejected about it.

"I advise you to look a little less happy," said the Ogre. "Our guests can be counted on to eat you." Then he went away downstairs, in a cloud of smoke, with the pipe still purring happily in his mouth.

"Oh, bother!" said Malcolm.

"Flipping *pest*!" said Johnny.

"Hard luck," Douglas said cheerfully. "Sorry we barged in like that, but our room's in rather a mess at the moment, and we didn't want him going in there."

"I think they've made a new discovery," Johnny said, as he and Caspar were getting into bed. "I wonder what. I know what I'm going to try for next."

"What?" said Caspar.

"Invisibility," said Johnny. "They can't make me be a waiter if I'm invisible, can they?"

Chapter 10

On Monday morning, the toffee-bars had finished Gwinny's sweaters and were bigger than ever. They had to give them Caspar's green sweater, after all, while they went to school. And, when Johnny came galloping up to their room that afternoon, eager to begin on his search for invisibility, to his great dismay, he met a toffee-bar half under the door, coming out. He collected it—with difficulty, for it was now more like a long heavy belt than anything else—and took it back to its box.

He told Caspar, and Caspar felt this was ominous. The green sweater was nearly all gone, too. They blocked the space under the door by doubling up comics and nailing them to the bottom of the door. While the Ogre was demanding from downstairs what that noise was, and they were trying to hammer the nails as quietly as possible, a peculiar and awful smell came to their nostrils. It was rather like the smell an electric fire makes when it has gone wrong, only ten times stronger.

They tracked it to the biscuit tins and Johnny took one of the lids off. "I think they're dead," he said, sadly surveying the motionless plastics.

Caspar knew they were. The smell proved it. Johnny might be sad, but Caspar could not help feeling relieved. It looked as if a number of the creatures had been growing wings before they died. Caspar thought of them all buzzing round the house and was thankful they had not had the chance. "You watch the toffee-bars," he said. "I'll go and bury these in the garden."

He staggered down with the pile of smelly tins and took them to the very furthest corner of the garden to bury. He was digging the hole, when he looked round to see the Ogre's pipe. It was watching him perkily from under a bush. It looked wonderfully healthy, glossy, and happy. Evidently being smoked agreed with it. Caspar made a fuss of it and offered it a dead, pink brick. It refused to eat it, but when Caspar's spade turned up a worm, the pipe pounced on that and ate it greedily.

"Then it's quite happy," Gwinny said, when Caspar told her. "Do you think the toffee-bars might be happy being eaten? That's what *they're* for, after all."

Somehow, neither Caspar nor Johnny felt like trying. So the toffee-bars continued to grow and thrive. On Tuesday morning they had to find all the cast-off trousers they could spare to make that day's food for them. After that, they supposed they would have to think of an excuse to ask Malcolm and Douglas for clothes.

Caspar came back that afternoon to find Johnny on the stairs, frantically struggling to hold back a huge whipping toffee-bar. "Help!" said Johnny.

Caspar cast down his schoolbags and came to Johnny's aid. They managed between them to catch the bar, and hauled it, flailing and resisting, back to their room. The comics had been torn aside from the door, all the trousers eaten, and some more carpet nibbled. Nine of the toffee-bars had draped themselves over the radiator above the box. Luckily, it was only lukewarm. Caspar and Johnny peeled them off it, despite their struggles. Caspar stood the box on its bottom and they thrust the toffee-bars into it. But they were now big enough to climb straight out again. They could only keep them in by covering the box with a Monopoly board and weighting that down with books.

"How many have we got?" Johnny said anxiously.

Caspar by now heartily hated the toffee-bars, and he did not care. "Hundreds."

"No, I think we've only got ten," said Johnny. "That means there are nine somewhere downstairs."

"Oh, my heavens!" said Caspar.

They found the toffee-bars in the Ogre's and Sally's bedroom. They must have gone there for warmth. The radiator there was the hottest in the house. Every one of those nine bars had draped itself over the radiator and melted on it. They were no longer creatures. Each was simply a strip of melted golden-brown toffee plastered flat to the radiator and oozing and trickling sluggishly onto the carpet. Johnny was near tears at the sight.

"Don't be an idiot!" Caspar snapped. "Start trying to get it off. I'll go and get a bucket of water and a scrubbing-brush."

Johnny mournfully knelt down in front of the radiator and began rather hopelessly picking at the toffee. Caspar dashed off down to the kitchen to get the fateful bucket and hurried upstairs again to the bathroom with the scrubbing-brush clattering about in the bottom of the bucket. He put the bucket in the bath and was just about to turn on the hot water, when he heard the Ogre coming upstairs.

Caspar's first impulse was to bolt the bathroom door and lie low. But he had left Johnny kneeling in front of the incriminating radiator. He knew he would have to go out onto the landing instead and distract the Ogre somehow. Caspar sighed. He went out onto the landing, perhaps not as swiftly as he might have done. And he was just in time to see the Ogre's back as he marched into the bedroom.

There was a silence. Caspar waited, nervously clutching the scrubbing-brush. The bedroom door was flung open. The Ogre, with his face distorted, shot out through it. He saw Caspar guiltily holding the brush, gave a snarl of fury, and grabbed at him. Caspar turned and raced upstairs for his bedroom. The Ogre pounded after him, much faster than Caspar had believed possible. Caspar climbed madly, and felt as if he was moving in slow motion. The Ogre climbed the stairs three at a time and seized Caspar's arm as he was rounding the bend. Caspar was so frightened that he used the judo-thing that should have brought him twisting out from under the Ogre's arm. But the Ogre proved unexpectedly resistant to judo. He lost his balance, but he hung on grimly. The result was that they both came heavily backward downstairs, in a sort of stumbling rush, just as Johnny, hoping to get clear while the Ogre was chasing Caspar, dodged out of the bedroom door with everyone's towels held to his chest in a wet bundle.

The Ogre, now thoroughly enraged, grabbed Johnny without letting go of Caspar and brought them together with a smash. Then he ran them into the bedroom, much as Douglas had run Caspar and Malcolm.

"Clean it," he said, putting them in front of the radiator. "Get rid of this mess before supper, or you go without. And you're not going to be a waiter tomorrow, Johnny, not even over my dead body!" He went straight upstairs and told Douglas he could be waiter instead. Douglas was not pleased. He came down and stood behind them as they labored.

"Can't you little squits keep out of trouble for one day?" he demanded. They did not answer. "Well, don't forget I owe you for this, too," said Douglas.

After that, Caspar tried to make Johnny get rid of the other ten toffee-bars. Sally's hurt and harrowed face when the Ogre showed her the mess made him hate them more than ever. It upset Johnny, too, but he would not part with the toffee-bars for all that.

"Then for heaven's sake make sure they can't get out," Caspar said, on Wednesday morning.

Johnny saw reason in this. They piled every book they had on top of the Monopoly board over the box, and left for school feeling they had done everything they could to keep the toffee-bars inside it.

They came home from school to the not quite unexpected sight of six enormous toffee-bars undulating down the stairs toward them.

Caspar and Johnny, without a word, each seized three and wondered where the others were. Malcolm was just behind them on the stairs and wanted to know what was going on.

"Nothing to do with you," panted Johnny.

"Because if—" Malcolm began.

But Sally came up behind Malcolm at that moment, saying, "Please, can I ask all of you to be very careful and quiet today, particularly this evening."

"Of course," called Caspar. He and Johnny mounted the

stairs as hard as they were able, with the toffee-bars beating like cart ropes in their arms. Malcolm had seen them by this time, and his eyes were wide. The only fortunate thing was that Malcolm was in Sally's way.

"What *are* you doing?" Sally said.

"Cleaning the stairs," gasped Johnny.

They opened the door of their room, threw the toffee-bars inside, and shut the door firmly on them.

"Well, don't make that kind of noise anymore," said Sally, arriving on the landing behind Malcolm. "Remember we're trying to give a grown-up party this evening. Malcolm, I think I'll need to press your suit. Can I get it?"

She and Malcolm went to the other room. Caspar and Johnny opened the door of theirs just in time to stop two of the toffee-bars coming out underneath it again. The books were scattered all over the room, and there was now a hole in one of Caspar's blankets. The four missing toffee-bars had draped themselves over the lukewarm radiator again. Caspar and Johnny once more peeled them off it and packed them into the box with the other six. Then they piled not only books, but cricket bats, train sets, rollerskates, and any other heavy things they could lay hands on onto the Monopoly board, until the heap stretched halfway up the wall. The box still heaved and bulged beneath it.

"Oh, this is *hopeless,* Johnny!" Caspar said, adding his pink football to the heap. "Please get rid of them."

By this time, Johnny was feeling much the same. But he wanted to be the one to suggest it. "I'll think about it," he said, and busied himself with the chemistry set.

Then Gwinny came in and looked at the heap and the

heaving box in undisguised alarm. "Johnny, you *must* get rid of them," she said.

But this only made Johnny obstinate. "They're only cold, poor things," he said. "They can't help it." And, after nearly an hour of arguing, he had managed to convince himself that he was sorry for the toffee-bars and had never wanted to get rid of them at all. "And they'd freeze in the garden," he said.

At that moment, Douglas thumped at the door and called out crossly. Caspar hurried to open it, in case Douglas came in and asked about the heap of things on the box. But Douglas did not attempt to come in. He simply stood on the landing looking worried and annoyed. "One of you's going to have to be waiter after all," he said. "Malcolm can't."

"Why not?" said Caspar.

Douglas hesitated. "Oh, come and look at him," he said at length. "Serve him right if you all laugh your heads off!"

They all trooped across the landing after Douglas, feeling very interested. Douglas flung open the door of the room and bowed to them as they went in.

"Lady and gentlemen," he said. "My brother, the— Hey, Malcolm! You were orange when I went out!"

"You didn't have to show everyone," Malcolm said uncomfortably.

He was a beautiful bright green all over, even his hair and his fingernails. His mouth and his eyes were a slightly darker green. He looked very peculiar indeed. But, while they were staring at him, quite confounded, he became more peculiar still. Another color seemed to be emerging through the green. At first they could not tell what color it was going to be. Then it spread slowly, stronger and stronger, like rings in water, or even more like the colored circles you see when you press your eyes, and turned out to be deep crimson.

"The green was quite pretty," Gwinny said, in some disappointment.

"How did you get like that?" said Caspar—and had a feeling he had said something like this before.

"Doing an experiment," the now crimson Malcolm admitted. He looked as if he had some dire disease.

"Stupid little ass!" said Douglas. "I'd warned you."

"You didn't do it on purpose, I suppose?" Johnny said suspiciously. "So as not to be a waiter."

Malcolm looked indignant and began, at the same time, to flush slowly indigo. "Of course not! It was something I was doing." He waved toward the table. Gwinny kept her eyes carefully on the experiment set up there, because Malcolm now looked as if he were turning into dark stone and it worried her. "I was just pouring in *Irid. col.,*" Malcolm explained, "and it splashed in my eye and I went blue."

"What were you doing?" said Johnny.

"Something complicated," said Malcolm. "Looking for invisibility, if you must know."

"Oh, so am I!" Johnny said in surprise. To Gwinny's relief, Malcolm began to turn yellow. She felt he looked more natural like that, even if it was a bright daffodil yellow. "Bet I find it first," said Johnny.

"Who cares?" said Douglas. "Which of you's going to be waiter?"

"It'll have to be me, I suppose," Caspar said reluctantly.

"Then go down and tell the Ogre," said Douglas. "I'll fix Sally."

"How?" said Caspar. "If she sees Malcolm like that, she'll have a fit. Hey! You called him the Ogre, too!"

"Well, he is, isn't he?" said Douglas. "And I'm going to tell Sally Malcolm's shamming ill in order not to be a waiter." Malcolm gave a cry of indignation and went lavender-colored. "Serve you right," Douglas said unfeelingly. "If you can think of any other way of stopping her coming to look at you, tell me."

Malcolm obviously could not. "Cheer up, Malcolm," Gwinny said, seeing how dejected he looked. "That's a really pretty color." Malcolm sighed. He was beginning to be a deep chestnut brown when Caspar left the room to find the Ogre.

The Ogre, with his pipe contentedly purring in his mouth, was in the dining room, moving the table. When Caspar came in, he said, "Take the other end and lift it over to the wall. Then go away."

While they were carrying the table, Caspar explained—rather haltingly—that Malcolm seemed to be ill. "So I think I'll have to be waiter instead," he said.

The Ogre put the table down with a thump. "No," he said. Caspar was intensely relieved. "You're bound to do something unspeakable," said the Ogre.

"I swear I won't," Caspar said unconvincingly.

"No," said the Ogre. "If you're there, all I'll be able to think of is what horrible thing you're going to do next. I'll make do with Douglas, thank you."

Caspar should have gone away at once after that. But he wanted to be able to assure Douglas that the Ogre refused whatever he said. So he said, "But if I promise—"

"Then you'll break that promise," said the Ogre, "as surely

as you'll break all the wine glasses."

Thankfully, Caspar turned to leave. But he had to stop rather suddenly as Sally hurried in with a tray of wine glasses.

"Don't bring those near Caspar!" said the Ogre.

Sally laughed. "Isn't it a pity Malcolm's unwell?" she said, and Caspar could see she knew Malcolm was perfectly all right. "But it's an ill wind. I rather like the idea of a representative from both sides. Don't you, Jack?"

The Ogre looked at her balefully. "All right," he said, to Caspar's dismay. "You win. But don't blame me if he wrecks everything."

"Does your suit still fit you, Caspar?" said Sally.

Three hours later, the lower part of the house had been feverishly cleared until it looked like somewhere completely different. Gwinny was hanging about outside the bathroom watching her mother put on make-up. Sally was wearing a silvery dress, and Gwinny could not take her eyes off it.

"Doesn't Mummy look beautiful?" she said to the Ogre. She was rather surprised to find he agreed.

Upstairs, Malcolm was turning from puce to mustard-color, and Johnny was anxiously watching the mound of things heaving above the toffee-bars. Downstairs in the kitchen, Caspar and Douglas, both feeling tight in the sleeve and constricted in the neck, were moodily standing by the trays and plates of food spread ready on the kitchen table. Caspar was feeling that Fate had played him a dirty trick. Douglas was worrying about Malcolm.

"Sally's bound to find out tomorrow," he said. "I don't know what to do."

"Have you tried washing his eye?" asked Caspar.

"I thought of that. It doesn't work. He *is* a stupid, careless idiot!" said Douglas.

"You sounded just like the Ogre when you said that," said Caspar.

"Are you trying to be funny?" growled Douglas.

"No," said Caspar, who was in no mood to be bullied. "Sometimes I'm surprised Malcolm even survives, the way you sit on him."

Douglas glared at him, which made him look like the Ogre, too. "If you—"

But the doorbell rang. Douglas had to hurry to let in a troop of cheerful guests. After them came more, and more. People filled the dining room and the sitting room, and then packed into the hall, where they stood shouting happily at one another. The Ogre pushed his way among them with bottles of wine, and both Douglas and Caspar were far too busy pushing their way after him with trays of food to think of being annoyed with one another for some time. Then they met again in the hall, where the noise seemed to be solid and Caspar could see nothing but people's backs. Caspar's head was aching, and he was hating being a waiter even more than he had thought he would. Nobody seemed to want food anyway.

The Ogre was pouring a drink for a lady standing at the foot of the stairs, and Douglas was just beside him. "Oh, are these your two sons?" the lady cried shrilly to the Ogre. The Ogre, who was too busy pouring wine to listen, nodded. "How nice!" exclaimed the lady. "I could see they were brothers. They look so much alike."

Douglas and Caspar looked at one another unlovingly over their trays. "This was all I needed!" Douglas said into Caspar's ear. "Fancy being taken for one of your family!"

"Same here," said Caspar. And it was annoying to see from the hall mirror that he and Douglas were, in fact, not unlike one another. Caspar turned away crossly from their reflections and saw a toffee-bar making its way downstairs.

Douglas had seen it, too. Caspar could tell from the expression on his face in the mirror when he turned back to balance his tray on the hall-stand. But Douglas said nothing. He simply held his tray of food persuasively out to the lady.

"Oh, those do look nice!" she said. "I oughtn't, you know. I'm supposed to be slimming."

While her attention was occupied, Caspar slipped round her and went flying up the stairs. He caught the toffee-bar on the fifth stair and lugged it on upward, raging.

Johnny was near the head of the next flight, looking absolutely desperate, wrestling with an octopus-like bundle of threshing toffee-bars. Malcolm, at that moment a startling shade of orange, was out on the landing holding another. He looked very nervous of it. It kept curling round his arm and he kept shaking it off.

"What on Earth do you mean, letting them out like this!" Caspar roared, with a ferocity which would have done credit to the Ogre.

"I can't *help* it!" panted Johnny. "They keep getting out whatever I do."

"Then get rid of them. Now. This moment," ordered Caspar. "This one was right down near the hall."

"How can I?" demanded Johnny. "I can't take them down through that beastly party, can I?"

Malcolm, flushing deep blue, suggested, "Why not throw

them out of the window?"

"I'm not going to hurt them!" Johnny said hysterically.

"All right," thundered Caspar, "if you're that soft, you can take them to the bathroom, put them in the bath, and run hot water on them until they melt. And do it *now*! You help him," he said to Malcolm, since Malcolm plainly knew all about it anyway.

"But—" said Malcolm.

"No, I—" began Johnny.

"Do as you're told!" Caspar howled at them. He slung the strayed toffee-bar at Malcolm and went rushing away downstairs to retrieve his tray before someone knocked it off the hall-stand. As he galloped downward, the noise and smell from the party rose about him in warm waves. As he rounded the last bend, he had a glimpse of Sally, looking very busy and pink and happy, pushing among the shouting people, and he realized the party was going very well. But suppose the toffee-bars got loose in it! It did not bear thinking of.

Douglas had rescued Caspar's tray. He was waiting at the bottom of the stairs as Caspar came hurtling down. "Here you are," he said. "That was one of the *Animal Spirits* things, wasn't it?"

"Yes," said Caspar, too distraught to wonder how he knew. "And that stupid little fool Johnny insisted on keeping them, and now they're all over the place!"

"What's he doing about them?"

"I told him to put them in the bath and melt them," Caspar said, rather pleased with his idea.

"Go back and tell him not to risk it," Douglas said urgently. "They'll swim like fish, if ours are anything to go by, and think how near the bathroom is! Go on. Go back and stop him. Hurry!"

He glanced nervously over his shoulder. Caspar looked, too, and found that the Ogre was pushing his way across the hall, obviously coming to ask what he and Douglas thought they were doing. But Douglas pushed Caspar toward the stairs and Caspar fled up them again, feeling the force of the Ogre's glare like a hot blast on his back.

When he arrived in the bathroom, it was full of steam. The plug was in the bath, the hot tap—which never ran properly—was trickling hot water, and Johnny and Malcolm were obediently lowering struggling toffee-bars into it.

"Take them out again," Caspar said breathlessly. "Douglas says they'll swim and not to risk it."

"Oh, blast Douglas!" said Johnny. "Malcolm's already told me that, and I'm *going* to risk it."

Caspar looked at Malcolm properly and found he was his right color again. "Thank goodness!" he said. "That's one thing gone right, at least. How do you know they'll swim?"

"Because all ours did," said Malcolm. "Douglas tried to drown the dustballs in Gwinny's room and the ones in ours, and he couldn't. Would you like to see them?"

"*No!*" bellowed Caspar. "Get those toffee-bars out. Throw them out of the window. And I'm sending Douglas up in five minutes to make sure you've done it!" Feeling extremely hectic, he pelted down into the roaring party again.

As soon as he had gone, Johnny said to Malcolm, "What do you mean, dustballs?"

"Just lumps of dust," said Malcolm. "At least, we think they were, but they grew. They look a little like mice now.

Shall I show you?"

"If you like," Johnny said, with alacrity. He took a look at the toffee-bars in the bath. They were evidently enjoying the warm water. Each bar was nestling down into it, and two were struggling for the place under the trickling tap. The water was already brownish with melted toffee. "Caspar can give orders all he likes," he said. "But you can see that's the kindest end for them. Come on."

He shut the bathroom door reverently and followed Malcolm up to his room. There, Malcolm opened the glass cupboard and showed him a shoe box on the bottom shelf. Huddled in it were six or seven grayish, fluffy lumps. Johnny was charmed. To his mind, they were even better than the toffee-bars. He admired them wholeheartedly.

Malcolm was obviously pleased by Johnny's admiration. "They're not bad," he admitted. "But they keep getting out. There used to be loads more." Then, as if he were letting Johnny into an even better secret, he said, "And these are my pencils."

Johnny, extremely flattered and quite lost in admiration, stared open-mouthed at the six pencils standing upright in a row on top of the cupboard. "What do they eat?"

"Wood-shavings," said Malcolm. "I have to keep sharpening ordinary pencils for them, or they eat the furniture. They only eat at night, too. They hop about and keep Douglas awake, and he throws things at them. That's how he knocked the *Animal Spirits* over and made the dustballs."

"But how did they get up to Gwinny's room?" said Johnny. "You said—"

"No. I made those," Malcolm said, looking a little self-conscious. "I spilled *Animal Spirits* in her room when I—when I was— Well, come and see, if you like."

So once again Johnny followed Malcolm upstairs. The noise of the party faded away behind them, and everything faded out of Johnny's mind except amazement at Malcolm's secret cleverness and acute curiosity about what he would see in Gwinny's room.

Gwinny was kneeling in the middle of her room cooking something in an old tobacco tin over the spirit-lamp from Malcolm's chemistry set. Seeing Johnny, she looked alarmed and rather guilty.

"It's all right," said Malcolm. "Can I show him the people?"

"If you want," Gwinny said cautiously.

Malcolm beckoned to Johnny. "Over here. But go quietly, because they get awfully angry if you frighten them."

Mystified, Johnny went to the place Malcolm showed him, to one side of Gwinny's dollhouse, and Gwinny watched him rather apprehensively while Malcolm leaned forward and gently eased off the front of the dollhouse. Johnny peered past him into its small dining room. The ten dollhouse dolls were sitting at the table, in the middle of eating supper. They were only too clearly alive. A number of them looked round irritably at the gap in the front of their house. Johnny could not help laughing at the expression on their faces.

Gwinny relaxed. "Are they ready for their pudding?" she asked.

"I think so," said Malcolm.

"Well, it won't be long," said Gwinny.

One of the men dolls left his chair and came to the gap. He pointed at Johnny and shouted something in a small grating voice that reminded Johnny of a tummy rumbling. Johnny laughed again, rather nervously.

"I don't understand their language," Gwinny explained. "But I think he means go away, they're having supper. Move over and let me give them this."

Johnny obediently moved, and watched, fascinated, while Gwinny spooned warmed-up custard into a tureen one of the women dolls fetched for her. He could not have described his thoughts. He felt he ought to be angry with Gwinny for making friends with Malcolm behind his back like this—except that he felt quite friendly toward Malcolm himself. He felt extremely honored to be shown all Malcolm's secrets, too. His only unpleasant feeling was a certain amount of envy. Malcolm had done such clever things with the *Animal Spirits*.

"I must get them a kitchen," said Gwinny. "They insist on a hot meal a day. But Malcolm lends me his lamp very kindly."

Malcolm was looking shyly at Johnny, to see what he thought of the people. "It's a terribly good idea," Johnny said. "I wish I'd thought of it."

"We didn't do anything as good as the Ogre's pipe," said Malcolm. "I thought Douglas was going to burst when he saw it."

"My people are quite as good!" Gwinny said indignantly.

"What else did you do?" asked Johnny.

Malcolm looked a little shamefaced. "Well—Douglas did it actually. He said it was to pay Caspar back."

"Did what?" Johnny asked suspiciously.

"I think I'd better show you," Malcolm said glumly, and got up.

Since Gwinny was quite as anxious as Johnny to know just what Douglas had done, she followed the boys downstairs, into the noise and smell of the party again. To their surprise, Malcolm took them into Johnny's and Caspar's room this time, and over to the cupboard.

"In here," he said, opening it. "You'll curse." Then he said, in considerable dismay, "Oh dear!"

Johnny thrust him aside and looked in. On the bottom shelf, comfortably curled up in the remains of Douglas's old sweater, were the two largest toffee-bars yet. They were the dark, treacly kind and had probably been the large seven-penny size to begin with. By now, they were as big as conger eels. And, in a wriggling heap beside them, were at least a dozen tiny toffee-bars, still too small to have cast their red and yellow wrappers.

"Oh!" exclaimed Gwinny. "They've had babies! How sweet!"

"*Sweet!*" Johnny said bitterly. All he could think about was the number of them. "Oh, *blast* Douglas! And I daren't tell Caspar. He'd go mad!" Talking of Caspar took his mind to other things. A troublesome thought struck him. "I say! Did I turn the bathwater off, or not?"

Caspar, meanwhile, was still trying to get hold of Douglas. He could see him in the doorway of the sitting room as he came downstairs. But Sally was at the foot of the stairs talking to the lady who thought he was Douglas's brother.

"Darling, what have you been doing?" she said. "Do, please, stop disappearing like this."

"Sorry," said Caspar. "It's the younger ones, really."

"Ah, you take your new responsibilities seriously, do you?"

said the lady, and made Caspar want to scream quietly.

He rescued his tray and set off toward where he had seen Douglas, but Sally said, "Not that way, Caspar. You go to the dining room."

Caspar pushed his way toward the dining room, meaning to go the other way as soon as he was out of sight. The more he thought about it, the less he trusted Johnny and Malcolm either to throw the toffee-bars out of a window or to melt them without letting most of them loose. Only Douglas, he felt, could see that they did it. And he thought he ought to set Douglas's mind at rest about Malcolm, too. But luck was against him. The Ogre was in the doorway of the dining room. He was not pleased with Caspar, and let him know it.

"Oh, are you with us again?" he said in a loud voice. "I'd hoped you'd gone for good." A number of people around the Ogre laughed heartily. Caspar thought it a typically mean and Ogrish thing to say. "They're shouting for food in the dining room," added the Ogre.

So Caspar was forced to go into the dining room without having found Douglas. He thought the best thing to do was to work his way to the other end, go out through the kitchen, and from the kitchen to the hall. But it took him some time. All the people packed into the dining room seemed ravenous for food, suddenly. They called Caspar this way and that and wanted to know if there were any sausages.

"I'll go and see," Caspar promised. He was more uneasy than ever, and he felt he simply had to find out what Johnny was up to. Leaving his nearly empty tray on the sideboard, he pushed his way to the other end of the dining room.

He had nearly fought his way to the kitchen door, when

something warm splashed on his wrist. It was followed by a warm wet splash on his nose. He looked up. Most of the people round Caspar were looking up, too, and looking annoyed. The reason was a brownish, spreading stain on the ceiling. It doubled in size while Caspar looked at it, and the drips came faster and faster.

Caspar dived for the kitchen door. The drips, at the same moment, turned into a waterfall. Water fairly thundered down. Sally opened the kitchen door, holding a tray of sausages. She and Caspar stared at one another through a steaming cascade.

"What's happening?" said Sally.

"I'll find out," said Caspar. He rushed through the waterfall into the kitchen and ran, steaming and gasping, into the hall. Water was coming through there, too, and he got another ducking, shut his eyes, and ran into Douglas coming the other way.

"What the—?"

"They've let the bath run over," said Caspar. "Come on."

He and Douglas struggled for the stairs. From the dining room came the sounds and smells of a tropical rainstorm. Sopping people, crying out with dismay, came surging out into the hall and made it difficult for the two boys to get through at all. When they reached the foot of the stairs, the lady who thought they were brothers was no longer there. Her place had been taken by a fat jolly man who playfully prevented them from getting by—unless the lady had turned into a man. Caspar felt anything was possible just then.

"What's going on, eh?" said the fat man, blocking the end of the stairs.

"Accident," said Douglas. "Please let us through."

"Reinforcements at hand! Taran-taran-tarar!" shouted the fat man and sat heavily on the bottom stair. They climbed over him desperately, and he tried to hit them as they went.

They pounded up the stairs and reached the bathroom at the same time as Johnny, Malcolm, and Gwinny. The door was open. The landing was a fog of steam. Through it, dimly, they saw the bathroom floor awash and the bath brimful of slightly toffee-colored water.

"You stupid little oaf!" Douglas thundered at Johnny.

"I told you not to!" bawled Caspar.

"I didn't mean—" said Johnny.

The Ogre breasted the steam and materialized in the bathroom door. He was carrying the back-brush. "Which of you did this?" he enquired in an unpleasantly quiet voice.

"Er," said Johnny. "Me."

"And me," said Malcolm bravely, though he was white with terror. "I distracted his attention at a crucial moment."

"Then," said the Ogre, "the rest of you get downstairs and pass out umbrellas or something. You two come in here."

Johnny found he had been right to postpone being hit by the Ogre. It was an exceedingly unpleasant experience. To Caspar's mind, the most unpleasant part was what the Ogre said to Sally after the last draggled guest had departed.

Chapter 11

Sally did not appear at breakfast the next day. "Your mother's feeling rather tired," the Ogre said, when Gwinny asked. No one was surprised.

The Ogre's idea of breakfast was thick, lumpy porridge, which he ate with salt and seemed to enjoy. No one else found it easy to eat, and Malcolm, who was looking white and ill, had none at all. And, as they set off for school, Caspar was positive he saw a toffee-bar crossing the sitting-room floor. It looked as if Johnny's disaster had not got rid of them, after all.

When Gwinny got home, the house was queerly silent. At first, she thought the queerness had to do with the stale wine smell left over from the party. Then it dawned on her that she could not hear Sally moving about anywhere. Sally always reached home before Gwinny did.

"She must be ill," Gwinny thought. "Poor Mummy, all alone ill all day."

She went quietly and considerately upstairs and softly opened her mother's bedroom door. The room was empty and the bed unmade. A heavy smell of toffee hung in the air. The reason, Gwinny saw, was that every remaining toffee-bar in the house had made for the warmth of this room's radiator and melted to death on it. More than half of them were

Douglas's dark ones. Parents and babies, too, had flocked to the radiator. Little red and yellow wrappers fluttered in the updraft or slowly slid down the sleepy, dark rivers of melting toffee. Pale toffee overlaid dark toffee, and dark toffee trickled on top of that. The radiator was fat with it, and it had dripped to the carpet in a dozen small growing mountains.

That must have upset Mummy, Gwinny thought. But she was too puzzled about where Sally could be to bother with the poor, silly toffee-bars. Sally was not in the still-damp bathroom, or in any other bedroom. She was nowhere downstairs. Gwinny went back to the toffee-scented room and thoughtfully opened Sally's wardrobe. The silvery party dress was hanging there, but most of the everyday clothes had gone.

With an anxious, heavy, foreboding feeling, Gwinny went downstairs to the Ogre's study and sat in the Ogre's leather chair to wait for the Ogre. After a minute, there was a slight clatter, and the Ogre's pipe hopped up from the garden onto the sill of the open window. It looked at Gwinny inquiringly. Gwinny stretched out a hand and made a fuss of it, but her heart was not in it. She was waiting. At length, the Ogre's car growled past the side of the house and crunched on the gravel. The door slammed. The Ogre's heavy footsteps filled the empty house. The pipe, knowing the sound, scuttled across to the pipe-rack on the desk and put itself there, ready to be smoked.

The Ogre opened the study door and came in, with his least likable expression on his face. "What do you think you're doing here?" he said when he saw Gwinny. "Get out."

Gwinny stood up. "Will you please tell me where Mummy is?" she said bravely.

The Ogre glowered. "She went to your grandmother's. She needed a rest."

"Oh," said Gwinny. "Did she go straight from work?"

"She did," said the Ogre. "Out."

Gwinny, very straight and upright, walked past him and along the hall. She knew something was not right. And she felt heavier and more anxious than ever. The front door opened as she reached the hall. Gwinny stood still and watched Caspar, Johnny, and Malcolm come in.

"Is something wrong?" Caspar said, seeing her face.

Gwinny nodded. "Mummy's gone. The Ogre said she's gone to Granny's straight from work."

All three looked at her in dismay. None of them were exactly surprised, remembering the expression on Sally's face the night before, and the things the Ogre had said to her. But it was odd.

"Why didn't she tell *us*?" Johnny said.

"I don't know," said Gwinny. "But I don't think the Ogre was telling the truth."

"Why not?" said Caspar.

"Because she hasn't made her bed," said Gwinny. "She always does." Johnny and Caspar looked at one another in alarm and bewilderment.

"You could check up," Malcolm suggested. "Does your grandmother have a phone?" He was very pale and tired-looking. Gwinny thought he might be ill.

"Are you all right?" she asked.

"Perfectly," said Malcolm.

Caspar threw down his schoolbags and seized the address-book by the telephone. He found the number and dialed.

"Where's the Ogre?"

"Study," said Gwinny. "Don't talk loud."

Granny answered the phone. "Caspar! Well, I never!" She was both surprised and delighted. "And how are you all?"

With his stomach sinking a little, Caspar said, "Fine, Granny. Has Mum arrived yet?"

"Your mother?" said Granny. "No, I've not seen Sally, dear. Why?"

Caspar did not quite know what to say after this. "Well," he explained hesitantly, "I thought she was supposed to be coming to see you straight from work."

"Oh, I *see!*" cried Granny. "Thank you for warning me, dear. Sally knows how I hate being taken by surprise. I'll go and put a cake in the oven for her. Thank you, dear. Good-bye." Since Caspar had no idea how to explain what he meant without alarming Granny thoroughly, he was thankful when she rang off.

"Well?" asked Johnny.

"Granny didn't know she was coming. But she might just not have got there yet," Caspar said, hoping for the best.

"Well, she ought to have done," said Gwinny. "Because I think she went this morning."

"So do I, now I think about it," said Malcolm.

They looked at one another, all thoroughly alarmed, wondering what this meant. And while they were standing in a group, staring, the front door opened again and Douglas came in. He stopped short when he saw the look on their faces. "What's up?" he said.

"Mummy's gone," said Gwinny. "And the Ogre told me a lie about where she was."

Douglas looked as dismayed as they were, and more dismayed still as they explained. "You have to hand it my father," he said at length. "He certainly has a knack of getting rid of his wives."

The story of Bluebeard burst into Johnny's head. "You don't think," he said, "that he's killed her and buried her at the end of the garden, do you?" Gwinny was horrified.

"Don't be a nit!" said Douglas. "People don't do that." Somehow, neither Gwinny nor Johnny was reassured by the way he said it. And, unfortunately, Caspar was too worried himself to think of backing Douglas up. So Gwinny and Johnny both gained a distinct impression that, if it had chanced to be the fashion to kill your wife and bury her at the end of the garden, Douglas would have expected the Ogre to do it. "You see," said Douglas, glancing at Malcolm. Then he saw how ill Malcolm was looking. "You'd better get to bed," he said.

"If you don't mind," Malcolm said politely, "I think I will."

At that, Caspar and Johnny noticed how poorly he seemed and loudly told him not to be a fool and to go to bed at once. Malcolm went away upstairs rather gladly.

"He always gets ill if people hit him," Douglas explained. "I was up half the night with him and——"

"Don't *you* hit him, then?" Caspar asked, in some surprise.

"Of course not!" Douglas said irritably. "But the point is, I think Sally may even have left last night. They had a flaming row, anyway. They were shouting at one another until after three o'clock."

"What about?" Johnny asked miserably.

"You, I think," said Douglas. "Then I heard Sally slamming

round the house afterward. And I don't think she was here this morning, whatever Father said."

"Then where do you think she went?" said Caspar.

"Couldn't tell you for toffee, I'm afraid," said Douglas.

Gwinny clapped her hands over her mouth. "Oh! The toffee-bars! They're all over that radiator again. I forgot."

"Oh *no*!" said Johnny.

They all streamed upstairs to look. The mess was, if possible, worse now. "Wow!" said Douglas, when he saw it.

"The ones you hid in our cupboard had babies, in case you didn't know," Johnny told him. Caspar was too depressed to do more than give Douglas a disgusted look.

"I'm sorry," said Douglas. "How was I to know they'd do this? We'd better get it cleared up before the Ogre sees it."

Nobody argued about that. Douglas fetched the fateful bucket again. Johnny brought six towels—Sally's was missing. Gwinny found soap and soda and washing-powder, and Caspar collected all the fluttering wrappers. Then they all set to work to peel the upper layers of toffee off the radiator.

The Ogre, alerted by the clattering of the bucket and the running of taps, appeared in the doorway while they were doing it. Johnny uttered a yelp of dismay. They all froze. "Who did it this time?" said the Ogre.

Since nobody exactly *had* done it, nobody answered.

"Are you here in an organizing capacity, Douglas?" the Ogre inquired. "Or have they corrupted you, too?"

Douglas went red. "It may surprise you to know," he said, "that it was at least half my fault."

The Ogre shook his head. "It doesn't surprise me at all. Johnny and Caspar could corrupt a saint. And I've had enough of them. I'm going to get rid of them if I can."

"Get rid of them?" Gwinny said, quite appalled. "Like you got rid of Mummy, you mean?"

"I *haven't* got rid of Sally," the Ogre said irritably.

"Then what have you done with her?" demanded Caspar. "You didn't tell Gwinny the truth, did you?"

"You lied," said Johnny.

"Yes, whatever you did, you'd no call to lie to them," Douglas said angrily.

The Ogre looked at their four defiant faces in the greatest surprise. He could not in the least understand why they should be so angry. It never once occurred to him that they needed to be told the truth. "You're all being quite ridiculous," he said. "Sally's simply gone away for a short holiday. You wretched children had tired her out between you."

"She hasn't gone to Granny, though," said Caspar. "And why didn't she tell *us*?"

"If you must know, she's gone to a hotel by the seaside," said the Ogre. "And she didn't tell you because she was sick and tired of you."

"Is that the truth this time?" Douglas demanded.

"Douglas," said the Ogre, "you may bully Malcolm, but you are not going to use that tone with me." They all knew at once from this that he had not told them the truth. And, if they needed anything more to complete their hatred and distrust of him, they had it in what he said next. "This is your fault, Caspar and Johnny," he said. "You two are destroying Sally's health, what with your water and your toffee and climbing on roofs, and I'm going to send you away to boarding school after Christmas to learn some decent behavior. I've had enough of you."

Caspar and Johnny were too appalled to speak. Douglas said, "That's quite unfair! It's just that these two haven't learned how not to be found out yet, and we have!"

"I take it you're asking to be sent away, too?" said the Ogre.

"No fear!" said Douglas, with deep feeling.

"Then don't provoke me," said the Ogre. "Get this revolting mess cleaned up, and then get down to the kitchen and find something we can eat."

It took them well over an hour to get all the toffee off the radiator. Then Douglas went down to the kitchen and did his best there. His best turned out to be large quantities of baked beans, which were stuck together in lumps, and also rather chilly.

"Is this all you could manage?" demanded the Ogre discontentedly.

"It's the only thing I know how to cook," Douglas explained.

Caspar, Johnny, and Gwinny were astonished at his ignorance. "We can all do bacon and eggs," said Caspar. "And Gwinny knows lots of things."

"Thank God!" said the Ogre. "Then put those beans back in the tins and do bacon and eggs."

They obeyed him. Gwinny thought that perhaps the beans would not keep in opened tins, so Caspar reheated them in the frying pan. "Go and ask Malcolm if he wants any," he told Johnny.

"Where is Malcolm?" asked the Ogre. "Buried in an experiment?"

"No, ill. And you haven't even noticed," said Douglas.

When Johnny went upstairs, he found Malcolm asleep,

with the six pencils standing on his pillow as if they were guarding him. His face was so wan and white that it quite worried Johnny. But Johnny felt it was no good telling the Ogre. The Ogre did not care two hoots whether any of them lived or died—with perhaps a bias in favor of their dying.

At this notion, the beginnings of an idea came into Johnny's head. He went over to the table, where Malcolm had left his chemistry set, and took a cautious look to see how Malcolm was getting on with his search for invisibility. To his pleasure, he found Malcolm had actually left a page of notes about it. Johnny, who carried everything comfortably jostling about in his head, was rather astonished by this, but he picked the paper up all the same. Then, feeling rather dishonorable, and keeping a wary eye on Malcolm's sleeping face, he read the notes through.

It was a list of the combinations Malcolm had tried, using one main ingredient from the lower layer and a number of other things, and an account of what he had done to each combination. One way and another, Johnny had tried two-thirds of them, too. The other third, Malcolm had now saved him doing. Better still, Malcolm had made two headings for his next experiments, which were to be with *Dens Drac.* and *Petr. Philos.*, both of which Johnny had already tried. Which left only *Noct. Vest.* that neither of them had tried. They were very close! Johnny promised to himself that he would make Malcolm a present of the formula when he had it, to make up for reading his notes, and crept out of the room.

"He's asleep," he reported downstairs.

"More for the rest of us," said the Ogre, with a total lack of feeling.

"You wait!" thought Johnny. "With any luck, you'll be in prison by Sunday."

Everyone ate the bacon and eggs with such gusto that Gwinny was hard put to it to find any spare food for her people. All she could collect was baked beans, bacon-rind, and a rather old tangerine. She put these things in a teacup and went upstairs to borrow Malcolm's spirit-lamp as usual.

Malcolm was still asleep, and the pencils were still standing guard on his pillow. Gwinny was alarmed at how pale his face was. She stood and looked at him for a while, and, the longer she looked, the more angry and motherly she felt about him. "But it's no good telling the Ogre," she thought. "He won't care." Besides, it was the Ogre who had made Malcolm ill by hitting him last night. He must have hit him awfully hard, Gwinny thought. Johnny had cried his eyes out. She stared at Malcolm's pale face, quite forgetting the damage he and Johnny had done between them, and the list of the Ogre's crimes grew longer in her head. After hitting the boys, the Ogre had done something dreadful to Sally—something so dreadful that he dared not tell them the truth. He was going to send Caspar and Johnny to a horrible school—Gwinny knew it must be horrible, since Douglas preferred to stay at home with the Ogre rather than be sent there. And now the Ogre did not care that Malcolm was ill.

It seemed to Gwinny that it was high time someone put the Ogre down, before he did anything else.

She squared her shoulders and went over to the chemistry set. The chemicals with the most poisonous names seemed to be *Noct. Vest.,* a nasty, spiky name, and *Petr. Philos.,* which sounded like the noise you made being sick. Gwinny took two fresh test-tubes and carefully poured two-thirds of each chemical into them. After that, with great consideration, she sharpened a heap of pencil-shavings onto Malcolm's pillow, so that his pencils should not disturb him by asking for food in the night. Then she took her test-tubes and the spirit-lamp away upstairs.

There was a scampering of dustballs as she opened her door. Gwinny was no longer afraid of them—as she had been when Malcolm first made them—but there were such a lot of them that they were a dreadful nuisance. They ran everywhere and ate her people's food. Her people had taken all her pins and needles to use as weapons against them. The dollhouse was in a state of siege this evening. The people would not let her open it, even when she had shooed the dustballs away. In the end, she had to hand them their baked beans on a teaspoon through their bedroom window.

"Oh dear!" Gwinny said. "I wish I had some rat poison."

This caused her to look at her two test-tubes again. *Petr. Philos.* had turned out to be little pieces of stone, rather like road chippings. She decided, on second thought, not to use it, in case the Ogre noticed it crunching in his teeth. So she took just *Noct. Vest.* downstairs with her.

Half an hour later, the smell of baking drew Douglas from the sitting room, where he was working in order not to disturb Malcolm, and Caspar from upstairs. Johnny was very busy with crucibles and would not leave them.

"Those look good!" Caspar exclaimed, as Gwinny carefully turned out twelve warm, golden buns onto a wire tray. He seized one and crammed it whole into his mouth. Douglas seized two and did the same.

Gwinny smiled as she went to the oven again. That meant her baking was sure to tempt the Ogre. Very carefully, she fetched out the thirteenth cake.

Douglas looked at it over her shoulder. "What's that?" he asked, with his mouth full.

"It's not for you," Gwinny said firmly.

"I should hope *not!*" said Douglas.

This cake was not golden, but gray. It had a hard, rocky look, and its surface glittered in an odd way. Gwinny had tried to make it look more edible by planting a cherry not quite in the middle.

Caspar looked at it critically. "If I were you," he said, "I should give that to the O—"

The Ogre, also attracted by the smell, came in at that moment. Gwinny, rather pink in the face, hastily put the gray cake back in the oven and shut the door on it. She had no wish to do her deed in public.

"Congratulations, Gwinny," said the Ogre with his mouth full, and went out again.

Douglas and Caspar stared outraged at the one bun remaining.

"He ate *eight!*" said Caspar.

"Isn't that typical?" said Douglas, but Gwinny only smiled.

As Caspar went back into his room, Johnny gave a cry of triumph and held up a piece of filter-paper with a hole in the middle.

"Got it! It's when you heat it up and let it go *cool* again."

"Got what?" said Caspar.

"Aha!" said Johnny. "Just try putting your finger through the hole in this paper, then you'll see."

He held the paper out in both hands toward Caspar. Caspar obligingly knelt down beside Johnny and put out a finger. To his surprise, his finger did not go straight through the hole. It met, instead, something which felt exactly like damp filter-paper. Almost unable to believe it, Caspar carefully ran his finger all over the blank space. It was astonishing. He could see Johnny's sweater through the space, but the hole was blocked with invisible, pulpy filter-paper.

"Good Lord!" he said. "It's invisible!" He took his finger away and found that the tip of it had gone slightly blurry. As he looked, the whole top joint blurred and then vanished. It had gone so completely that Caspar could not help taking a quick look down at his finger from top view. He had half-expected to see a cross-section of bone and flesh. But it simply looked pink. Gingerly, he touched the space where the missing top joint should have been. And he could feel it still there.

"I wish you hadn't done that!" Johnny said crossly.

"Why?" said Caspar, who was beginning to feel rather pleased with it.

"Because the Ogre's bound to notice."

"The Ogre wouldn't notice if I stuck it in his eye," said Caspar. "And do let's think about where Mum's gone now. She must be somewhere."

But Johnny did not seem to want to discuss Sally. "It's the Ogre's fault," he said. "And he'll pay for it. You wait." Then somewhat to Caspar's surprise, he packed up his chemistry set and went to bed.

Since Caspar was also rather tired, he, too, went to bed early, and then lay awake a long time wondering where Sally was, why she had gone, and why the Ogre would not tell them. Then he thought of sixteen totally unlikely ways of finding her. And, finally, he began dismally wondering whether boarding school was as dreadful as he feared. The only comfort he could see was that Malcolm had survived one. And that was not very comforting.

Chapter 12

As soon as he was quite sure that Caspar was asleep at last, Johnny got up again and dressed. Stealthily, in the dark, he felt about and found the test-tube he had put out ready. Carefully, quietly, feeling his way by the wall, he crept downstairs to the bathroom. Only when he had the door safely locked did he dare turn on a light. He sighed with relief then, and turned on the hot tap to its smallest, quietest trickle. As soon as it was running properly hot, he put the plug in the bath and began shaking the powder from the test-tube into the hot trickle, until he had about four inches of clear, steaming, lilac-colored liquid. Then he turned the tap off and sat down on the clothes basket to wait for the liquid to cool. He was determined to do this properly, and he knew it was going to be a long job.

Gwinny, meanwhile, tossed and turned in her bed. The scutterings of the dustballs kept waking her up, and in between she had terrible dreams. The first time she woke up she told herself she did not repent of her crime—not in the least. All she had done, after all, was to rid the world of an Ogre, quickly and quite kindly. The others would say she had done right. And they might even wish they had thought of it, too.

The second time she woke up, the cistern in the loft was making a great deal of noise, almost more than the dustballs. This was Johnny's doing, but Gwinny thought it must be the Ogre having a bath. And that meant the Ogre had not gone to bed yet and not yet eaten the cake. Gwinny knew she would have to lie and listen for the dreadful moment when he did. She had left the cake on his bedside table, with a doily under it to make it look prettier, and she had sort of made his bed, to give him the idea she was looking after him now that Sally was gone. But, in the dark, with the cistern running and the dustballs scuffling, Gwinny began to think that this had been deceitful of her. She had no business to let the Ogre think she liked him enough to make his bed and give him cakes. But she had to admit she could hardly have got him to eat the gray cake any other way. So she covered her head with the bedclothes, in order not to hear when he came out of the bathroom, and fell asleep.

The third time she woke up, the dustballs were running about in droves, squeaking. And Gwinny started up, with the most vivid memory of all the things she had put in the gray cake. They were more than even an Ogre's stomach could bear. Gwinny could see, before her in the dark, a vision of the Ogre clutching his stomach and rolling in agony. It was awful. In her efforts to finish him off quickly, she had been most horribly unkind. She knew it now. She just had to get up and see if he was dead yet—and if he was not, she would have to wake Douglas and ask him to put the Ogre out of his misery.

Gwinny did not like the dark, particularly not with a corpse in the house. She switched on lights as she crept downstairs, until she came to the door of the Ogre's bedroom. She did not quite like to turn on the light in the room itself, so she pushed the door wide open to let the light from the landing shine in.

As she did so, the Ogre gave the most dreadful, rattling groan.

Gwinny stopped in the doorway, appalled. She could see the Ogre quite clearly. He was lying on his back, not moving. But his mouth was open and, as Gwinny peered forward, out of it came another rattling groan. Just to make quite sure, Gwinny crept into the room. The cake was gone, right enough. The doily was still there, but the Ogre had eaten the cake, thinking Gwinny was being kind, and now he was dying in his sleep. It was terrible. He groaned for a third time.

"Oh, wake up! Wake up!" Gwinny said frantically. Now she knew what she had done, she wanted to stop it at once. But she dared not touch the Ogre in case she finished him off completely. She dared not call Douglas. And when the Ogre groaned yet again, she dared do nothing except wonder how she came to be so wicked. "Oh dear!" Gwinny said, hovering round the edge of the bed. "Oh dear! Oh dear! Oh dear!"

The Ogre shut his mouth on another groan, rolled over, and switched on the bedside light. "Oh, it's you!" he said crossly. "What on earth are you doing at this time of night?"

Gwinny stared at him, confounded. He was blinking and tousled, and clearly in none too good a temper, but he seemed nothing like dead. Perhaps the poison took a long time to work after all. "Do you think you could make yourself go sick?" Gwinny said earnestly.

"No, I could not," said the Ogre. "Whatever for?"

"Because you may not know it, but you're awfully ill," said Gwinny. "You were making the most terrible groans in your sleep just now—"

The Ogre sighed. "Groans?" he said. "Oh, I shall never understand children! Go back to bed, Gwinny. I was only snoring. I'm not in the least ill."

"Yes, you are!" Gwinny said, wringing her hands. "You ate my cake and you're going to die!"

A shade of alarm entered the Ogre's sleepy face. "I ate eight," he said. Then a reassuring thought struck him. "And Douglas and Caspar ate the rest, but they're all right, aren't they?"

"Not those, stupid!" Gwinny said. "My special gray cake that I put beside your bed to poison you!" The Ogre looked completely blank. Feeling she was never going to convince him, Gwinny pointed to the empty doily. "You must have eaten it. It's gone. It was on that. And you're going to die and I don't want you to!" she said, bursting into tears.

The Ogre, looking exceedingly alarmed, got hastily out of bed. "What did you put in this gray cake, Gwinny?" But now Gwinny had started crying she was quite unable to stop. The Ogre had to take hold of her and shake her slightly, and ask her again, before she could answer.

"I put," she sobbed, "I put *Noct. Vest.* out of Malcolm's chemistry set."

"Well, that's supposed to be nontoxic," said the Ogre. "Maybe there's no harm done."

"But I put six of Mummy's sleeping pills squashed-up in it," continued Gwinny, "and detergent and the bottle from the cupboard that says *Poison* and some firelighter and ammonia, and then I rolled it on the floor to get germs and spat on it for more germs, and instead of sugar on the outside I put the burning kind of soda. And I think it ended up awfully poisonous."

By the end of this list, the Ogre's face was almost as gray as the cake had been. "My God!" he said faintly. "I think it did!" But as Gwinny burst into renewed sobs, he said, "And I haven't eaten it. Gwinny, are you listening? I've not seen it. It certainly wasn't here when I came to bed. Are you sure you put it here, really?"

"Of course I did," wept Gwinny. "You must have seen it."

"No, I haven't," insisted the Ogre. "So you see what that means, don't you? Someone else in the house must have eaten it."

This possibility had never occurred to Gwinny. She cried harder than ever. "Not Caspar or Douglas," she said. "They didn't like the looks of it."

"That leaves Malcolm and Johnny," the Ogre said anxiously. "Oh, lord! Malcolm didn't have any supper, did he?"

"Oh no!" wept Gwinny, quite horrified at the idea. "He was asleep!"

"And what's to prevent him waking up hungry?" asked the Ogre. "Gwinny, don't you understand—?" He stopped and listened. It sounded to her like the water running out of the bath and someone at the same time quietly easing back the bolt. "I think your victim may be in the bathroom at the moment," said the Ogre. "Wait here." He got up and went out to the landing. Gwinny, most anxious, followed him as far as the doorway. The Ogre waited for whoever it was to open the bathroom door. When no one did, he opened it himself.

The bathroom was in darkness. The Ogre, as puzzled as Gwinny was, leaned inside and switched on the light.

"No one here," said the Ogre, scratching his head a little.

He went into the bathroom to make sure.

As soon as he moved from the doorway, Gwinny heard someone come through it. Someone crossed the landing— she felt the wind they made and the slight warmth of them— and hurried with quiet, invisible footsteps upstairs. After that, the Ogre might be puzzled enough to lie down and look under the bath, but Gwinny knew that either Johnny or Malcolm had found out how to make himself invisible. Struck by a sudden, beautiful hope, she scampered back to the Ogre's bedside. She put out her hand and felt the doily. And never had she been more relieved in her life. The cake was there. Hard as a rock and gritty as granite, it was there under her fingers. She had simply made it invisible somehow.

Heartily thankful, Gwinny put out both hands to it and picked it up. It was heavy as a stone. She hurried with it to the wastepaper basket and opened her hands above it. The invisible cake fell with a thump that rocked the wastepaper basket and scattered toffee-wrappers. Gwinny was rubbing her hands on her nightdress to get rid of the invisible soda, when the Ogre came back, looking extremely sleepy and thoroughly puzzled.

"I could have sworn—" he said.

"I found the cake!" Gwinny said, pointing triumphantly. "It's here, in your wastepaper basket. Somebody threw it away."

She prayed that the Ogre would not come and look. Luckily, he was far too sleepy, and he could see from her sudden cheerfulness that she was speaking the truth. He sat heavily down on the bed. "Thank heaven for that! Now come over here, Gwinny, and tell me what made you decide to poison me."

Gwinny began to cry again at this, and she approached very reluctantly indeed. It was some time before she was perched on the bed also, as far away from the Ogre as she could be. It was difficult to explain, too. "Well," she began, at last. "You're so horrible, you see."

"I am?" said the Ogre dismally. "A promising beginning. Go on."

Gwinny twiddled her toes for encouragement, and went on. "Always fussing about noise and never letting anyone do anything and making everyone afraid of you. But I'd sort of got used to that. But then you hit Johnny and hit him, and hit Malcolm so that he was ill. And you got rid of Mummy and told lies about it, and Johnny thinks you buried her at the end of the garden, and Douglas almost agreed, but I think you must have done it farther afield than that. Now you're going to get rid of Johnny and Caspar, too—"

"Only send them to school," the Ogre protested, sounding rather depressed.

"But they go to school, anyway," Gwinny pointed out. "You just want them out of the way because they disturb you a lot. And Douglas would rather live with you than go to boarding school, so you can see what it's like. But it was mostly because of what you did to Mummy and Malcolm that I decided to put you down."

This finished what Gwinny had to say, so she stopped. A silence followed. Gwinny could not help looking nervously sideways at the Ogre. She expected to see his face distorted with rage, but, in fact, he just looked tired and gloomy and seemed to be deep in thought. She sat twiddling her toes, until the Ogre asked, rather cautiously, "Are you going to have another shot at putting me down?"

"No. It's too wicked," Gwinny said sadly. "I found out it was when I saw you groaning."

The Ogre seemed relieved. "You know," he said, "Sally said that if you kids chose to murder me she wouldn't blame you, but I didn't think she meant it literally."

"She didn't tell me to," Gwinny said. "I thought of it myself."

"I know that," said the Ogre. "You don't really think I murdered Sally, do you?"

Gwinny hooked one big toe behind the other and considered. "Not quite," she said. "Douglas said people didn't—but there was a murder on the news last week, so you could have done. Why did you tell lies, if you didn't?"

"Well, you don't expect me to tell you children all about something that was private between Sally and me, do you!" the Ogre retorted. "Sally's left. That's all you need to know."

"No, it isn't!" Gwinny said passionately, with tears quivering out of her eyes again. "If Mummy's gone, it's private between *us,* too!"

There was another short silence, while the Ogre considered this. "I suppose you have a point," he admitted. "All right. I don't know where Sally's gone. I spent most of today trying to find out. We had a terrific quarrel, which started about the bathwater and went on to other things, and Sally left about three o'clock on Thursday morning. Does that satisfy you?"

"Yes," said Gwinny. "No. Isn't she coming back?"

The Ogre sighed. "Only to collect you five children. She'd have taken you then, except you were asleep at the time. Now she's trying to find somewhere for you all to live—I think.

And I must say, if you can think I—" The Ogre seemed to come to the end of what he had to say, too. There was a pause, in which Gwinny, somewhat comforted by the thought that Sally might be coming back to fetch her, sniffed and tried to stop crying. Then the Ogre said, as if he had made up his mind about something, "Look here, Gwinny, I seem to remember you used to like me at the beginning. Tell me truthfully—haven't you let Caspar and Johnny influence you? Don't you think you may have let them build me up in your mind as a—as a sort of ogre?"

This was not easy. Gwinny went rather pink at the way he put it. "A bit of both," she admitted. "I mean, I was angry about Malcolm, too."

"Now, Sally talked about Malcolm," the Ogre said thoughtfully.

"Malcolm's nice," said Gwinny.

"He's a complete mystery to me," the Ogre said frankly. "All right—I'll do my best to understand Malcolm, if you can promise me to give up poisoning for good. What do you say?"

"Yes," said Gwinny.

"Good. And," continued the Ogre, as if he were not so certain of what came next, "it might be possible to be friends again, don't you think? If we were, we'd have a much better chance of persuading Sally to come back."

"Do you want Mummy back?" Gwinny asked, in some surprise.

"Of course I do!" said the Ogre, equally surprised that she should ask.

Gwinny began to cry again. The Ogre was being so kind that she was ashamed. She was overwhelmed with her wickedness in trying to poison him, worse than when she had thought he was dying, and far more than she would have been if he had been angry and fierce. "I'm sorry," she sobbed. "I'll be nice to you now. I promise I'll try."

"And I'll try, too," said the Ogre. "Look, I think you're tired—and I know I am. Suppose you come back to bed?"

Gwinny nodded and slid to the floor. "But Caspar and Johnny—" she said.

"Don't worry about them," the Ogre said cheerfully. "When Sally hears they're going to school and not at home to wear her out, she'll be all the readier to come back."

Gwinny was dubious about this, but she was too tired to argue. Now that the Ogre had talked of being tired, she found her head was nodding forward.

"Come on," said the Ogre and picked her up. Gwinny had not been carried for years. She had thought she was too old. But it was such a pleasantly trouble-free way of going upstairs that, far from protesting, she fell asleep on the way. She woke up a little when the dustballs scuttered, because the Ogre said, "We seem to have mice."

"Not quite mice," Gwinny said, as she was put on her bed, and went to sleep without hearing the Ogre's answer.

Chapter 13

Caspar was mildly surprised next morning when Johnny was not there. But he supposed Johnny must have got up early for some reason, and simply got on with the oddly difficult task of dressing with one finger-joint invisible. As long as he did not look at what he was doing, it was all right. But, whenever he actually watched his fingers working on buttons and shoelaces, he miscalculated. His eyes kept telling him he lacked the usual length of finger and he kept believing them. It gave him an unusual, angry, frustrated feeling.

He met Malcolm on the landing when he had at last finished. "Are you all right?" Caspar asked.

Malcolm nodded—he looked unusually jolly—and they went downstairs together. "Johnny left me a note," Malcolm said. "He's gone to school already."

"He must be mad!" said Caspar.

On the lower landing, Douglas was just going into the bathroom with a dirty shirt. The Ogre, looking half asleep and more than usually terrifying, came stumbling out of his room and caught him at it. "What do you think you're doing with that?" he said.

"Putting it to be washed," Douglas said, evidently wondering if the Ogre was mad.

"Take it upstairs and put it on again," growled the Ogre. "How the devil do you think things are going to get washed with Sally not here? By magic?"

"I've already put on a clean one," Douglas said patiently. "I'll be late if I have to change."

"Then don't dare do it again!" said the Ogre. "No one is to change anything until they've worn it at least a week." He went stumping away downstairs. Douglas turned to Malcolm and Caspar, and to Gwinny, who was yawning her way downstairs behind them, and expressively tapped his forehead.

In the kitchen, there were the remains of Johnny's breakfast. His schoolbag and coat were missing, too. Caspar did not realize that anything was wrong until someone asked him at lunchtime where Johnny was. After that, he could hardly wait to get home and see what Johnny was up to.

Douglas, Malcolm, and Gwinny seemed in the same hurry to get home. They all four entered the musty and depressing house at the same moment. The hall was alive with little gray, fluffy things, which scuttered and squeaked and ran from their feet. They could see dustballs climbing chairs in the sitting room and running round on the dining-room table. There seemed more of them in the dining room than anywhere else.

"Oh dear!" said Malcolm.

"Your dustballs seem to have taken over where our toffee-bars left off," said Caspar. "Why are they all over the place like this?"

Douglas marched over to the dining room, sending dustballs scurrying in droves from under his feet. "Somebody's been feeding them," he said. They crowded behind him at the dining room door. On the dining-room floor were a dozen or so bowls and plates, each with a few corn flakes still in them. From the rate the dustballs were eating the corn flakes, it was easy to see that they had not been put down so very long ago.

"I bet it was Johnny," said Gwinny.

Caspar was astonished by the vast numbers of the dustballs. "You never had all these in your room, did you?"

"We did," said Malcolm. "We had them the day the Ogre tried to smoke his pipe. But they were smaller then. Do you think if we put the corn flakes out in the garden and opened the back door, they'd all go outside?"

They tried it. But the dustballs evidently did not like the cold air outside. A few came to the back door and no further. Most of them came only to the middle of the kitchen.

"Hopeless," said Douglas. "Leave them. I'll ring up a rat catcher. Caspar, are all of Sally's friends in that address-book by the telephone?"

"I think so. Why?" asked Caspar.

"I thought I'd have a go at finding her," said Douglas. "She must be *somewhere*, and one of them might know. I thought I'd ring—"

The telephone rang at that moment. Both Caspar and Douglas ran to answer it, both thinking it might be Sally. Douglas won, by pushing Caspar at the last moment, and picked up the receiver. An agitated voice quacked.

"Yes, Mrs. Anderson," said Douglas. It was Granny. Caspar hopped from one foot to the other. He could tell by the way Granny's voice quacked on and on that Sally certainly had not gone to Granny's and Granny was worried stiff by this time. "No—you see, Mrs. Anderson—" Douglas said several times, but he could not get another word in for quite a while. At last he said loudly, "*No.* It's quite all right. I'd fetch her, only she's out shopping at the moment. Caspar got the wrong end of the stick. It's *next* week she's coming." Then he let Granny quack about how relieved she was and rang off.

"That was brilliant!" said Caspar, genuinely admiring.

"Except that now we've *got* to find Sally," said Douglas, picking up the address-book. A dustball leapt off it and ran away across the hall. "And a rat catcher," said Douglas. "We'd better call them rats, hadn't we?"

Gwinny, meanwhile, inspired by her new friendship with the Ogre, was doing what she had hurried home to do. She collected all the dirty clothes from the bathroom and took them to the kitchen. There, she sorted them carefully and put them into the washing machine with soap-powder. It was only when she turned to the controls of the machine to switch it on that she realized she had not the faintest idea how it worked. Still, she was determined to be a help to the Ogre, so she hunted for the instructions on the shelf above the washing machine. The vacuum cleaner lived on this shelf. Gwinny found instructions for it. She found a cookbook and Johnny's schoolbag hidden there. But when she finally laid hands on the booklet that went with the washing machine, it seemed to be written in Spanish. She gave up and yelled for Caspar.

Caspar came, but was quite as ignorant. He took hold of a knob and tried turning it. It came off in his hand.

Gwinny snatched it and crammed it back on. "Now look what you've done! Go and get me Malcolm. He'll find out. Or Johnny. Johnny knows how to work it. Where *is* Johnny anyway?"

"Somewhere about," said Caspar, and went upstairs to find Malcolm. "Gwinny can't work the washing machine," he told Malcolm. "Can you?"

"I expect I can find out," said Malcolm. He left off carefully heating *Noct. Vest.,* which was what he had hurried home to do, and went downstairs to try.

Caspar, at last, went into his room. And he stopped just inside the door, appalled. Johnny's bed was torn asunder. Its sheets trailed on the floor, and, in the middle of the bottom sheet, was a large pool of blood. The carving knife lay across Johnny's pillow, also covered with blood. And, on the wall above the bed, a desperate hand appeared to have clawed five long streaks of blood. Below that, the same hand had written, also in blood, the word *OGRE,* and the *E* of it fell away into a trail—as if the writer of it had been at his last gasp. Johnny had been both artistic and thorough. Caspar felt a little sick. If he had not known Johnny had been feeding dustballs half an hour ago, he might have thought Johnny had indeed met with a singularly gruesome end.

As it was, he understood what had happened. Feeling rather glad that the Ogre had not come in yet, Caspar laughed—somewhat hysterically—and went downstairs to fetch Douglas. The Ogre came in at the moment he reached the hall, and Douglas hurriedly put the phone down.

"Mice!" said the Ogre, staring at the scampering dustballs.

"I've just rung up for a rat catcher," said Douglas.

"Good," said the Ogre. "Though I should think the Pied Piper would be more use. Where's Gwinny?"

"In the kitchen," said Caspar, and signaled Douglas frantically to come upstairs.

Douglas turned quite pale when he saw Johnny's bed. "Where did he get all that blood from?" he said. "And where *is* he?"

"Invisible," said Caspar. "And I think the blood's off that meat in the bottom of the fridge. It has the same sort of smell."

Douglas drew a deep breath, perhaps to smell the blood, perhaps because he was feeling sick. "Let's get rid of it, anyway," he said. "Or the Ogre might really murder him."

Caspar, glad to find Douglas exactly agreed with his own feelings, went and dragged at the gory sheets, while Douglas heaved the blankets clear.

Behind them, Johnny's voice said peremptorily, *"Leave it alone!"*

They spun round and faced the empty room.

"You're not to touch it!" Johnny said out of thin air. "What do you think I did it for? Ring up the police and get him arrested. Go on."

"Don't be a silly little twit!" Douglas said scornfully. "They'll know it's only animal's blood. If you wanted to do it properly, you should have used your own blood."

There was a hurt silence from the empty part of the room. Douglas and Caspar dragged the sheets from the bed, took off the pillowcase, and picked up the grisly knife. Then Johnny spoke again:

"All right, you rotten spoil-sports! I'm going to try Plan B. I wish I'd tried that first now."

"Get that blood off the wall before you start, then," said Douglas.

"Do it yourself, if you want it off," Johnny retorted. Douglas dived for where his voice came from, but missed him completely. And, as Johnny made no further sound, neither of them could tell whether he was still in the room or not.

"This is going to be real fun and games," Douglas said, as they trailed the gory sheets downstairs. "What do you think Plan B is?"

Caspar had no idea. But he felt he would not put anything past Johnny. He was out to get the Ogre and, as he was invisible, get him he surely would. If the Ogre had been anyone else, Caspar would have felt sorry for him.

The Ogre himself was in the kitchen translating the book of instructions for Malcolm, while Malcolm tried to make the washing machine work. They had managed to get it to fill itself with water, but nothing else, and they refused to let Caspar put the sheets in it. So Douglas wrapped them in a bundle, blood-side inward, and dumped them in a corner to wait. They tried to warn Gwinny not to unwrap them, but she was gazing enchantedly at a dollhouse kitchen the Ogre had bought her and would not listen.

"My people will love this!" was all she would say.

Feeling extremely harassed, Douglas and Caspar fetched the fateful bucket again, to clean the blood off the wall.

"Is Johnny at it again?" said the Ogre, hearing it clanking. "Try pressing the third from the left, Malcolm."

When Douglas and Caspar came down again, the washing machine was working. The Ogre, Malcolm, and Gwinny were all admiring it. An hour later, they were not admiring it so much. An hour later still, they were not admiring it at all and wondering how to stop it. By this time, it had washed and rinsed and washed again, on Malcolm's reckoning, seventeen whole times, and seemed set to go on all night. Caspar, who was feeling rather hungry by then, went to the larder and looked for food. All he could find was baked beans.

"I say," Douglas said to him, under the noise of rinsing and spinning. "Does Johnny know how that thing works?"

"Yes," said Caspar, "now I come to think of it."

"Then I think he's sitting on top of it pressing switches down," said Douglas.

They both went to see if this was true. At the same moment, the Ogre lost patience with the washing machine and tore its plug out of the wall. The turning and rinsing stopped, to the relief of everyone. Then the Ogre, in spite of Malcolm and Gwinny loudly telling him not to, rashly bent down to open the front.

This was the moment Johnny had been waiting for. Everyone except the Ogre saw the vacuum cleaner lurch up from the shelf over the washing machine. They saw it whirl round on its hose and come whistling down toward the Ogre's head. Without a word, Gwinny, Malcolm, and Caspar threw themselves sideways at the Ogre, and Douglas hurled himself at the space beneath the vacuum cleaner. The vacuum cleaner crashed to the floor. Everyone, with the Ogre underneath and Caspar on top, toppled into a spout of cold water and washing and lay for a moment weltering. Nobody knew where Johnny was. But the vacuum cleaner ended up under the kitchen table, a most peculiar shape.

The Ogre threw the rest of them off and arose, red-faced and dripping. *"What the—!"* he began at full roar. Then he caught Gwinny's eye and changed to speaking quietly. "Why did you do that?"

"We were trying to stop you opening the washing machine,"

Malcolm said in a shaking voice. He and Gwinny did not need to be told what was happening. And everyone felt the same: Johnny had gone too far.

The Ogre looked round at their four frightened faces. "It's all right," he said. "It was entirely my fault. You told me not to open it. Fetch me the fateful bucket, one of you."

Douglas and Caspar squelched off to get it. They could see a line of wet footprints leading to the hall, where Johnny had made off.

"Has he gone mad?" Douglas whispered.

"No," said Caspar. "He just hates the Ogre."

"Well, I thought I hated him, too," said Douglas. "But I'm almost sorry for him now. What's got into Johnny, if he isn't mad?"

"I think it's being invisible," said Caspar. "I've been feeling peculiar all day with the top of one finger gone—so think how much worse he's feeling."

Douglas gave Caspar's shortened finger a hunted sort of look. "We can't go on like this," he said. "We won't know where to look for Johnny next."

"*Bucket!*" yelled the Ogre.

"*Coming!*" bawled Douglas. Then he whispered to Caspar, "We'll have to think up some way to get the Ogre out of the house while we round up Johnny. Think hard."

That was all very well, Caspar thought, going out into the hall among the scampering dustballs, but what excuse would take the Ogre out of the house without supper? Particularly as it was now raining. Raindrops pattered on the glass over the front door, and the hall was dark. Caspar switched on the light. He saw the telephone receiver in mid-air and the dial spinning.

"Drop that, Johnny!" Caspar sped to the telephone. It was clear to him that Johnny was now trying to ring the police and report himself dead.

The receiver plummeted to the end of its cord and swung there. Caspar heard Johnny scudding toward the stairs. He clapped the receiver back on its rest and kept his hand on it, wondering whether to cut the cord. Short of a day and night guard on the telephone, he could see no other way of stopping Johnny carrying out what was presumably Plan C.

"You mean pest!" said Johnny's voice.

"Please stop, Johnny," Caspar said. "Everyone else thinks you're mad. I know you hate the Ogre, but—"

"You keep stopping me, and he hasn't even noticed I'm not here!" Johnny said fiercely. "You may not care that he's got rid of Mum, but I *do*. And I'm going to get him for it—even if you *are* all on his side!"

"We're *not* on his side," said Caspar. "You just can't bash people's heads with vacuum cleaners."

"Yes, you can," said Johnny. "I did. If you hadn't—"

But, in the kitchen, Malcolm had come up with an idea to get the Ogre out of the house. Damp and harassed, the Ogre hurried into the hall. "Caspar," he said, "Malcolm's saying Johnny's run away. Do you know anything about it?"

Caspar mentally took his hat off to Malcolm. "We—er—we think he may have gone before breakfast," he said, hoping that this tallied with what Malcolm had said.

The Ogre forgot all consideration for Gwinny and thundered, "WHAT?!" at the top of his voice. In the echoing silence that followed, Caspar heard Johnny's feet flitting upstairs.

"We were hoping you wouldn't notice," Caspar said uncomfortably.

The Ogre glared at him, and then at Douglas, Malcolm, and Gwinny, who came trooping out of the kitchen to see how the idea was going. "You stupid little idiots!" said the Ogre. "Why didn't you tell me at once? Where's he gone? Do you know?"

Under the anxious eyes of the other three, Caspar cast about for somewhere extremely far off. "Scotland," he said. "He—we—our great-aunt lives there. And she doesn't have a phone," he added hastily, as the Ogre strode toward the telephone. "She lives in a very remote thingummy—er—glen, I mean."

"I see," said the Ogre dourly. "Do you happen to know the way to this remote glen?"

Behind the Ogre, Douglas nodded vigorously, to show Caspar what to say next. "Yes," said Caspar, and tried to remember where Loch Lomond was on a map—this being the only place in Scotland that came into his head.

"Very well," said the Ogre. "Get a raincoat, unless you're wet enough already, and come out to the car. We'd better go there."

This was not at all what anyone had intended. In considerable dismay, Caspar slowly collected the coat that he had dropped on the dining-room floor, very much hoping the Ogre would change his mind. But he did not.

"Hurry up!" he said, getting into his own coat.

Caspar was forced to put on his coat and follow the Ogre to the back door, past the glum line of the other three. He jerked his thumb up as he went, to show them where he thought Johnny now was, and went apprehensively across the wet floor of the kitchen and out into the wetter night. Cold rain drove into his face and pattered on the car when he was inside it. It was not a very good night for going all the way to Scotland in, Caspar had to admit.

He watched the Ogre start the engine and switch on the headlights and wipers. His stomach fluttered. Going to Scotland might be all right, but what to do when they got there was another matter. Caspar thought he ought to let the Ogre get as far as Perth or Dundee or somewhere, and then remember another great-aunt in Fishguard or Land's End where Johnny might have gone. Then he could think of another somewhere else, perhaps, and so work the Ogre back home. He saw he was in for a very difficult night.

Chapter 14

The Ogre backed the car into the road and turned it with a wet smicker of tires. "Not quite the night I would have chosen for driving to Scotland," he remarked. Since Caspar thoroughly agreed, he said nothing. The Ogre joined the nearest northbound road. "I seem to have had no sleep lately," he said plaintively. "If we crash, blame Johnny, not me." There seemed no reply Caspar could make to this, either. He sat in silence, inventing great-aunts, until they came to the main road north, full of wet squiggles of light and dim orange rain. "This is horrible," said the Ogre. "How far do we go on this wild-goose chase?"

A nasty collapsing feeling came into the pit of Caspar's stomach. "Why is it a wild-goose chase?" he said.

"Because I know Johnny's at home," said the Ogre. "I distinctly heard his feet on the stairs, and I think I heard his voice in the hall just before that. Would you mind telling me what's going on?"

"Nothing!" Caspar said. "You made a mistake. He's not at home, really. He may be in Land's End, though."

"With another great-aunt?" said the Ogre.

"Yes," Caspar said uneasily.

The Ogre braked, with a shriek of wet tires. Tires screamed

behind them, and horns honked. "I'm too tired to drive round the British Isles all night," he said. "I'm going home."

"No!" Caspar said frantically. "Please!"

"Why?" said the Ogre. The car stopped by the side of the road, and other cars went by, flashing their lights and honking indignantly.

"Because Johnny might kill you," said Caspar. "Or get you arrested for killing him."

"Oh no! Not another!" exclaimed the Ogre. "And you brought the carving knife with you, I suppose."

"Of course not!" said Caspar. "What do you take me for?"

"I don't know," said the Ogre. "I gave up trying to understand any of you months ago—and I know that was stupid of me, so don't tell me. I'll find a lay-by and you tell me about Johnny."

He drove slowly on again. Caspar saw the game was up and that he would have to explain in some way. He wished he knew how. If Malcolm had been there, he might have thought of something. Caspar could only think of the truth and, as he thought it, he realized he dared say nothing unless he made sure Johnny was not in the car, too. He was forced to turn round and grope at the back seat to see if it was empty.

"What are you doing?" the Ogre asked suspiciously.

"Making sure Johnny's not in the car," Caspar explained.

The Ogre turned into a lay-by and stopped with a jerk. "All right," he said wearily, turning on the light in the car. "There. If he *is* here, he's invisible."

"He *is* invisible," said Caspar. To be on the safe side, he climbed over into the back and felt all round it. To his relief, it really was as empty as it looked.

The Ogre, who was watching him in the mirror, sighed. "This is a very pretty pantomime," he said. "Perhaps the invisible great-aunts are there, too."

"Oh, shut up!" said Caspar. "You wouldn't joke about it if you knew how Johnny nearly got you with the vacuum cleaner just now. If you don't believe me, take a look at my finger." He scrambled back and thrust his hand under the Ogre's nose. "And it does awfully peculiar things to your mind," he added angrily.

The Ogre gave Caspar's hand an irritable look, but, when he saw that one finger really was shorter than it should be, he seized Caspar's wrist and looked closer. Then he ran his finger and thumb along Caspar's finger until they closed on the invisible joint at the end. "Good grief!" he said. "It's there!" He was very shaken. Caspar could tell he was, though the expression on the Ogre's face was its normal grim one. It occurred to Caspar that the Ogre's face was not good at showing feelings, just like Malcolm's. "This process," said the Ogre, still holding Caspar's unseen fingertip. "Could it work on other things? Cakes, for example?"

"I expect so," said Caspar. "It works on filter-paper and Johnny's clothes."

"Ye gods!" said the Ogre. "And I thought she'd simply had a nightmare!" Instead of explaining what he was talking about, he let go of Caspar's finger and said, "All right. How did it happen?"

"Well, you know those chemistry sets," Caspar began. Since it seemed easiest to start at the beginning, he told the Ogre about the flying-powder. That of course led to Malcolm shrinking and the way Douglas had gone heavy in the road.

Caspar, now he knew how bad the Ogre's face was at showing feelings, thought the Ogre seemed a little ashamed at the way he had misjudged Douglas, but the Ogre did not interrupt him until Caspar was halfway through explaining *Misc. Pulv.* Then Caspar was startled to find the Ogre glaring at him.

"Look here," said the Ogre. "Were you and Malcolm actually changed over that day I met you in the shop? It's all right. I'm not going to eat you."

Caspar let go of the back of the car seat, which he had grabbed for safety. "Yes. We wanted the antidote, but you bought us pink footballs."

"You must have blessed me for that!" said the Ogre. "How did you get back—or are you really Malcolm now?"

"No," said Caspar. "Douglas did it." As he said it, he found himself comparing the Ogre with Douglas. They were really remarkably alike. And the thing about Douglas, Caspar now knew, was that though he seemed ferocious and loved ordering people about, he did it because he could not help it, and there was no harm in him, really. Perhaps the Ogre was the same. Certainly, he was not being nearly as angry at the tale of crimes Caspar had to tell as Caspar had expected. Caspar went on to explain the *Animal Spirits* with a growing, guilty suspicion that he had been misjudging the Ogre horribly.

He hoped the Ogre was believing him, but the Ogre's face remained somber and grim, and Caspar could not tell. Yet, as Caspar pointed out, the Ogre had tried to light a living pipe, had twice seen the toffee-bars on the radiator, and had met the dustballs in the hall that very evening. But the Ogre gave no sign of what he thought, even when Caspar told him about Johnny's bed, and the vacuum cleaner, and Plan C.

"So we had to get you out of the house while we rounded him up," he said. "You do believe me, don't you?"

"Oh yes," said the Ogre. "You're the worst liar I know. That's why I brought you along. You think being invisible has gone to Johnny's head, do you?"

Caspar made an effort to explain. "A bit. But I think mostly he doesn't feel like *him* anymore—he's a sort of angry ghost."

The Ogre thought. "I see. And what is he most angry about? Sally leaving?"

"Yes," said Caspar. "But about boarding school, too, and now us getting together to stop him getting you."

"Does he think I murdered Sally?" asked the Ogre.

It had not occurred to Caspar up to then that Johnny could think anything so silly, but, now the Ogre mentioned it, it did seem possible. "I—I think he might," he said awkwardly. "He's young enough to think stupid things."

The Ogre was acutely depressed. Even his face showed it. "What an ogre you must think I am!" he said.

"Oh no!" Caspar said hastily, in the greatest embarrassment. "It's just us—not trying to understand you."

"The same goes for me," said the Ogre ruefully. "Well, all I can think of is that we do what Douglas did, and go and ask the old man for the antidote. Failing that, we get Malcolm to experiment, at the risk of turning himself into a teaspoon or something." He put out his hand to start the car again.

"No, don't!" said Caspar. "It isn't safe to go back. Honestly."

"Listen, Caspar," said the Ogre, "this is very kind of you, but I don't like what you've told me about the effects of invisibility at all. It sounds as if Johnny has become all thoughts, and nothing else. And they were angry thoughts to begin with.

I think he might harm himself even more than he can harm me. And another thing—I'm pretty sure he's been invisible now for nearly twenty-four hours, and if we leave him much longer he may be warped for life. Now do you see?"

"Yes," said Caspar soberly.

The Ogre started the car and made a U-turn out of the lay-by, in front of another row of indignant, hooting, flashing motorists, and drove back much faster than they had come. "Do you think," he asked, peering between the swatting wipers and the driving rain, "that it might help bring Johnny to reason if I promised not to send him to boarding school?"

"Yes, it would," said Caspar. He sighed, rather, and thought it was just his luck that he should be the only one being sent.

"There's no need to sound so dismal," the Ogre said, as they reached the outskirts of town. "If Johnny's to be at home, I shall have to keep you, too, as a Johnny-tamer. And, anyway, I can ill spare the money."

Caspar grinned with relief all the way to Market Street. "I say," he said then. "Don't let on to Malcolm I told you about *Irid. Col.* and the other things, will you? He'd be awfully upset."

The Ogre promised not to say a word, and drove into the little dark yard. "Wait here," he said, and hurried away to the shop. Caspar sat in the car, waiting, worrying rather about Johnny, but mostly thinking how stupid he had been to be so much afraid of the Ogre all this time. Then he saw the Ogre coming back and eagerly wound down the window. At the sight of the Ogre's face, however, he had to grip the edge of the window hard and remind himself that the Ogre was like Douglas and not as fierce as he seemed. But the Ogre was not angry with Caspar. "What a very unpleasant old fellow that is!" he said. "He laughed his head off at our misfortunes."

"Didn't he tell you the antidote?" Caspar asked, wondering what on Earth they would do.

"Yes, when I threatened to wring his neck," said the Ogre. "Plain water is the answer. When did you last wash your hands, Caspar?"

Caspar was not sure. The last time he clearly remembered was when Sally had insisted on it, just before the party. But surely he could not have mopped the blood off Johnny's wall and then weltered in the washing without getting his hands wet! He put his hand out of the window into the rain to see. Sure enough, as soon as his hand was thoroughly covered in raindrops, a pink fuzz appeared at the end of his shortened finger, and in no time at all it was fully visible. His familiar fingernail glistened under the street lights, and Caspar was very glad to see it again.

"Not since last night, evidently," said the Ogre, getting into the car. "Now let's go and get out that fateful bucket."

But they did not need to. When the car approached the house, they saw Malcolm on the other side of the road, soaking wet and waving the mop. Gwinny was in the middle of the road with the broom, and Douglas was posted in the gateway, making menacing passes with a rake. They could all be clearly seen in the drizzle drifting under the street lights. And, in the space into which the broom, the mop and the rake were pointing, was the misty, speckled shape of Johnny, slowly being washed visible again by the rain.

The Ogre stopped the car with a squealing jerk. He leaped out of it, seized the fuzzy shape by its collar, and took it away into the house. The other three, panting rather, gathered round the car.

"I had to tell him everything," Caspar said apologetically out of the window.

"I was afraid you would," said Douglas. "Can't be helped." In fact, he and Gwinny and Malcolm were too pleased at the way they had rounded Johnny up and restored him to think of much else. They all told Caspar at once how Malcolm had seen the soles of Johnny's shoes when Johnny fled from the stream of washing. That had given them their clue, but it had taken a deal of hard work and cunning to drive Johnny out into the rain. They had only just got him there before the Ogre came back.

"I think we ought to make sure the Ogre doesn't hurt Johnny too much," said Gwinny, at length.

They went indoors. But the Ogre and Johnny were in the study. Since no sounds of violence were coming through the door, no one quite liked to interrupt. It seemed as if they were simply talking. They never found out what was said in there, but, when Johnny came out about half an hour later, he did not seem at all unhappy. He looked a little sober, perhaps, but in a sort of way he looked rather smug, too. The Ogre, on the other hand, looked tired to death. Caspar looked from one to the other and guessed that Johnny had extorted a number of promises from the Ogre. Johnny was rather good at turning things to his own advantage. Caspar sighed, and foresaw that in the future it would be his duty to defend the Ogre from Johnny—if he could.

"We're awfully hungry," said Gwinny.

"Baked beans?" suggested the Ogre.

Everyone shuddered, and half of them groaned.

"Oh, very well," said the Ogre. He felt in his pockets and produced a five-pound note. "Can someone find a fish-and-chip shop open, then?"

Five hands snatched at the note. Douglas, naturally, won and held it high above his head. "Then mind you get me sausages," said Malcolm.

"I like fish-cakes," said Gwinny.

"And at least a mountain of chips," said Johnny.

Douglas duly returned with a bulging carrier bag, which they dismembered on the kitchen table. The smell was so delicious that the Ogre's pipe struggled out of his pocket and showed an active interest in the sausages. The Ogre watched it nervously.

"I shall never bring myself to smoke that again," he said.

"But you must! It likes it!" Caspar protested.

So, when the vast meal was over, the Ogre dubiously picked the pipe up and put some tobacco in it. The pipe at once went stiff and began purring. Encouraged by this, the Ogre packed it properly and lit it. And shortly, he had almost forgotten it was alive. "Go and get me these chemistry sets," he said. "Now. As the car's still out, I'm going to take them back to that unpleasant old man, before anything else happens."

Grudgingly, Johnny and Malcolm obeyed. Reluctantly, they brought the sets to the kitchen and wistfully handed them over. And the Ogre got up from the littered table and took them back to the shop there and then. Everyone felt rather flat without them.

"Nothing will ever be the same again," Gwinny said sadly.

"You've still got your people," Malcolm reminded her.

"Oh, good heavens!" exclaimed Gwinny. "I never gave them their supper!" She hurried busily away at once with a handful of leftover chips.

Chapter 15

Nobody really blamed the Ogre for staying in bed the next morning. They found themselves breakfast. Then Caspar went upstairs and was just dropping the stylus onto his favorite Indigo Rubber track, when he remembered the Ogre was still asleep and took the record off again. It was just as well, because Douglas came in the next minute.

"Come on," he said. "Let's find Sally while the coast's clear."

He and Caspar fetched two of the chairs from the sitting room to the hall and sat in them while they went methodically through the address-book. They took it in turns to telephone every soul in the book and ask them if they knew where Sally was. They had only got to B, when the doorbell rang. Douglas bawled to Gwinny to answer it.

The visitor was a man from the Council who told Gwinny he was the Rodent Operative. She and Malcolm and Johnny showed him the dustballs. They thought he was rather a nice man. He looked shrewdly at the scuttering, fluffy shapes.

"One of you's been breeding a fancy kind of mouse here and let it get out, haven't you?" he said. "I know children."

They followed him from place to place round the house,

watching with interest as he spooned out what looked like porridge oats with an old ladle and poured a little heap of the stuff in every corner.

"Don't any of you touch this, mind," he said. "It's poison. Dries them up and kills them."

This alarmed Gwinny. She was afraid her people might take it for porridge and eat it. So, as soon as the Rodent Operative had gone, she got Malcolm and Johnny to help her write out twenty-two cards, saying *DANGER*. They stuck the cards to matches and the matches into empty spools and put each notice beside one of the heaps of poison. Gwinny was not sure her people could read English, but she hoped they would get the idea all the same.

They were putting out the notices when Douglas and Caspar heard the Ogre come out of his bedroom.

"Take these chairs back," Douglas said, with the receiver at his ear. "Then keep him away from here."

Caspar trundled the chairs through the sitting room doorway and shut the door on them. When the Ogre stumbled downstairs in his dressing-gown, Caspar met him at the foot of the stairs and hurried him away to the kitchen before he could ask what Douglas was doing. There he fed the Ogre solicitously with tea and pieces of charred toast.

"Very kind of you," said the Ogre. "If I wasn't so tired, I'd wonder what your motive was. Those blessed dustballs kept me awake half the night. Has the rat catcher been here?"

"Yes," said Caspar, pointing to the heap of poison in the corner. "But Malcolm says you have to call him a Rodent Operative."

The Ogre blinked sleepily at the pile of poison and Gwinny's notice in front of it. "Why are you warning them?" he asked. "To give them a sporting chance?"

Caspar could not help laughing. "Gwinny did that," he said. But he felt rather guilty, now that he knew the Ogre better. The Ogre liked making jokes. But he always made them with a perfectly straight face. Caspar feared that they had taken him seriously on a lot of occasions when he had only meant to be funny. "I'm sorry about the toast," he said apologetically, "only the dustballs ate the other end of the loaf, so I couldn't make any more."

"I've heard charcoal's good for indigestion," the Ogre said philosophically, and poured himself another cup of tea to help the toast down. Caspar was rather touched, because he saw that the Ogre was determined to behave well. He was wondering whether to go out and buy some more bread, when Douglas burst jubilantly into the kitchen. And so determined was the Ogre to behave well, that he did nothing but glower faintly.

"I've found her!" boomed Douglas, beaming with triumph.

"Found who?" the Ogre asked wearily.

"Sally, of course!" said Douglas. "She's—"

The Ogre jumped up so hastily that his chair fell over and Caspar had to pick it up. "How on Earth did you manage that?"

"I rang up everyone in the address-book. And Aunt Joan told me."

"And I rang Joan twice!" the Ogre said, in considerable disgust. "Where *is* Sally?"

"You'll never believe it—with Aunt Marion! She—"

"Don't tell me!" said the Ogre. "Joan and Marion thought

it would teach me a lesson. Why did I take those chemistry sets back? I would have enjoyed turning Joan or Marion into a rather small hippopotamus. Did you ring Marion?"

"Yes, and I talked to Sally. She—"

The Ogre hastened to the door and shoved Douglas aside. "Let me get to that phone!" But there he stopped and seemed puzzled. "What are *you* doing, wanting Sally back?" he asked Douglas. "I thought you were the anti-Sally party."

Douglas went red. "Yes—I know," he said. "But that was because I didn't like all the *change,* really. Then the kids were so upset when she went, and—and I felt it was rather my fault she'd gone, because she tried like mad to be friends and I wouldn't be."

"You relieve my mind," said the Ogre. "I thought it was my fault. How do you rate the chances of getting her back?"

"I keep trying to tell you!" said Douglas. "She said she can't get here till about four o'clock, but—"

"You mean she's coming *today?* Oh my God!" said the Ogre. "Look at the state this house is in!"

There followed some hours of hectic work. Malcolm and Johnny, who were busy wiring batteries to the dollhouse cooker so that Gwinny's people could cook for themselves, were reluctant to stop, even for Sally. But Gwinny swore she would pull the wires out again unless they helped. She made them carry dollhouse and people out into the garden, to be away from the dust. Then everyone began work. It was hard work, because the vacuum cleaner proved to be broken and they had to manage without, but in the end the house gleamed and shone. No dust or dustballs remained. Even Johnny's and Caspar's room was tidy, and the dustbins so full that their lids stood like hats, several feet too high, on top of wedged-down rubbish. The mop and the broom, which had both suffered much herding the invisible Johnny the night before, fell to pieces with use. The Ogre said they had better buy new ones, and another dustbin, too.

"And some more baked beans, while we're at it," he said looking round the empty larder.

Though Caspar knew this was only a joke, no one trusted the Ogre to go shopping. They all said they would go, too, and crammed themselves into the car. There Malcolm produced pencil and paper, rested the paper on Caspar's back, and made a list of essentials. It began with tinned salmon, because Malcolm liked it, and went on to caviar, because Gwinny said she had never had any.

"Put down porridge," said the Ogre.

"Two dozen doughnuts, Malcolm," said Johnny.

While the Ogre drove toward the shopping center and the list lengthened, a curious smell began to fill the packed car. Caspar sniffed. It reminded him disturbingly of some of the smells Johnny had produced with the chemistry set. Douglas was sniffing, too. They exchanged glances. But, for the moment, the main worry was the shopping list. Douglas took it away from Malcolm.

"We don't want," he said, crossing things out vigorously, "salmon, caviar, porridge, peanuts, or more than a dozen doughnuts. But you haven't put in sandwich spread." And he put it in.

"Why sandwich spread, just because *you* like it?" Johnny demanded belligerently. "Why can't Malcolm have salmon?"

"Douglas," said the Ogre, "stop being so domineering and

allow each of us one luxury. Mine's porridge. Gwinny can have caviar if she insists—though, honestly, Gwinny, you'd be better off with crisps—and then we'll buy a few optional extras like eggs, bread, and butter."

"Do I get more crisps for the same money?" asked Gwinny.

"About a hundred times more," said Caspar.

"Then put me down for crisps," said Gwinny.

The list was adjusted accordingly, and Caspar thought of tea just as they reached the shopping center. The Ogre turned into the big gravelled parking area and found a space over in the far corner. They opened the doors and piled out. While the Ogre was locking the car, Douglas pounced on Johnny and Malcolm.

"You've kept some of those chemicals, haven't you? Hand them over."

Johnny and Malcolm looked sulkily at one another, and then from Caspar to the Ogre, hoping for some support against Douglas. But Caspar heartily supported Douglas and said so, and the Ogre at that moment happened to be half inside the car locking the far door.

After a second, Malcolm fetched a small vial from his pocket. "Oh, all right!" he said. "It was only *Dens Drac.,* because I haven't tried that yet."

"So's mine!" Johnny said in surprise. Having given himself away in this manner, Johnny was also forced to yield up his vial. Its stopper was cracked, which accounted for the smell.

"Typical!" Douglas said disgustedly. "Don't you both realize we've all had *enough* of that!" He took both vials and hurled them away into the lane between the parked cars. Both burst as they hit the ground. Johnny and Malcolm miserably watched the white grains inside soak away into the wet gravel.

The Ogre came out of the car in time to see what Douglas had done. "That was rather uncalled-for," he said. "Have you considered the effect of broken glass on car tires? Go and pick up the bits." And, when Douglas had grudgingly done so, the Ogre sent him with Johnny to the hardware store while the rest of them went to buy food. "I'm not having either of you handle groceries with whatever that is on your hands," he said.

Johnny and Douglas set off. Johnny was very resentful. Whatever Caspar said, it seemed to him that Douglas had no right to order him about. And he told Douglas so, several times.

"Oh, all *right!*" Douglas said at length. "I'm sorry. Are you satisfied now?"

"No," said Johnny. "You'd no call to break my *Dens Drac.*"

"And what do you think you'd have done with it if I hadn't?" said Douglas. "Made some awful mess, I bet."

"I shall never know now, shall I?" Johnny pointed out.

When they reached the hardware store, however, they stopped arguing about the *Dens Drac.* in order to argue about whether to get an orange plastic dustbin or a shiny metal one. And, having decided on the metal one, they disputed brooms, then mops.

"Sally likes them to match," said Douglas. "I know she does."

"Just because you do," said Johnny. "I say, let's get her a present, shall we?"

Quite suddenly, he and Douglas were overwhelmed with excitement that Sally was really coming back. They bought the first mop at hand. Then, without disputing at all, they went to the shop next door and pooled their money for a cake of soap shaped like a strawberry, which pleased them both very much. Douglas put it in the dustbin and carried that and the broom back to the car. Johnny marched beside him carrying the mop like a lance, with the dustbin lid for a shield.

To their annoyance, they were first back to the car. It was locked and deserted. They were wondering what to do with the dustbin while they went to look for the others, when Douglas said:

"Hey, look! Mushrooms or something."

It was in the spot where he had broken the vials. Several large round, white things were pushing up through the gravel, definitely growing. They did almost seem to be giant mushrooms. Douglas and Johnny were so intrigued by them that they dragged the dustbin over there to have a look. Whatever they were, there were nearly fifty of them, bulging and pressing up from the ground like big solid bubbles. One or two of them had lines or strips of black-and-white squares across them.

"You know," Johnny said, laughing a little, "they almost look like crash helmets."

"They do, rather," Douglas agreed. "I wonder what they are." Cautiously, he stretched out the broom and tapped the top of the nearest. It gave out a hard, solid rapping—exactly the noise you would expect from hitting a crash helmet with a broomstick.

The thing—whatever it was—objected to being rapped. It shook angrily, scattering gravel. The next second, it had grown to a complete sphere, and there was a face in the front of it. It was not a pleasant face, either. It was a coarse, sly, aggressive face, and it glared at them.

"It *is* a crash helmet!" exclaimed Johnny. "What's he doing buried in the ground like that?"

They stared at the buried man in some perplexity, wondering how he got there and whether to help him out. While they stared, the face shook its chin free of sand and stones and spoke. "Ἰτμιον θε λιδαγειν ἀνσε υο 'τιυγετ!" it said.

"What language is that?" said Johnny.

"It might be Greek," Douglas guessed, equally mystified.

A clattering of gravel made them look up. The other mushrooms, up and down the lane between the cars, had also grown into men in crash helmets. The next nearest was now only buried from the waist downward. He had his hands on the gravel and was levering to get his legs free. Beyond him, a number had grown to full height and were stepping up onto the ground, shaking their boots. They were all identically dressed in black leather motorcycle suits and white crash helmets, and they all had most unpleasant faces.

With one accord, Douglas and Johnny looked round to see how near the car was. It was twenty yards off. Between them and it, the lane was filled with motorcyclists stepping free of the ground and moving menacingly down toward them.

"I don't like the look of this," said Douglas. "And don't tell me it's my fault. I know."

The nearest man struggled up from the earth and shook himself. Stones clattered from his leather clothes and mud spattered the boys. Carefully he drew his boot from the last of the gravel and walked a step or so toward them. "Θινκ ἰυ κυιτ φελλως ὁν θε ἐδ δουιου?" he demanded of Douglas.

"I'm sorry. I don't understand," Douglas said.

The man looked round at the other motorcyclists. "Θης κιζ τραιδ του θυμπ μι φελλως!" he said angrily.

From the way the others reacted, it was clear that, whatever this meant, it meant no good for Johnny and Douglas. They all gave the boys most unpleasant, blank looks and strolled nearer. "Ωκει, λετς τεικ βωθοφεμ ἀπαρτ ἀβιτ," said one. And one who was still only half out of the ground added, "Λετμι ἀττεμ." Neither of these suggestions sounded pleasant. Johnny looked despairingly round what he could see of the car-park between the advancing leather suits. He found nothing but cars, lines of them, locked, silent and deserted. There did not seem to be another soul in sight.

"Get back to back," said Douglas. "Use the mop on them."

Johnny at once scrambled round Douglas and leaned against his back. He held the dustbin lid as a genuine shield, and put the head of the mop under one arm, with the stick pointing outward toward what was now a circle of menacing motorcyclists. Behind him, he heard the clang of the strawberry soap rolling in the dustbin as Douglas raised that for a shield and leveled the broom. Johnny was glad that he had such a tall back as Douglas's to stand against. If it had been Caspar's or Malcolm's back, he would have felt a great deal more frightened.

Not that their defenses seemed to impress the motorcyclists. Some laughed jeeringly. One said, "Φυλλα σπιριτ, ἀρντθει?" which was clearly a sarcastic remark of some kind, and all of them laughed.

Then the first of them said, "Λετσγω, φελλως." And they closed in. Johnny found his mop gripped and twisted, and hung on to it desperately. Behind him, Douglas braced his back against Johnny's and hung on to the broom. Several more motorcyclists converged casually and quietly from the sides.

"*Help!*" shouted Johnny.

The Ogre, walking heavily under an enormous cardboard box, led the others up the next lane by mistake. Near the end of it, he stood on tiptoe to look for the right lane. "Sorry," he said. "It's over there. What's going on in that lane?"

Caspar put his box on a convenient car bonnet and stood on its bumper to see. "Those look like Hell's Angels," he said.

"They do," agreed the Ogre. "Perhaps we should wait till they go."

But at that moment, Johnny shouted for help from the middle of the bunch of black-leather bodies. Then Douglas shouted, too. Caspar hastily picked up his box, and all four of them edged between the cars as quickly as they could, until they came out beside the Ogre's car in the right lane. Beyond, near the fence of the car-park, the fight was heaving. Clangs and exclamations came out of it.

"Oh, they're horrible!" said Gwinny. "What shall we do?"

"It isn't Hell's Angels," said Malcolm, "exactly. It's that stuff Douglas spilled. Look."

They looked, and saw the last motorcyclist growing and struggling out of the ground, obviously in the most tremendous hurry to join in with the others.

"What was it called?" asked the Ogre.

"*Dens Drac.,*" said Caspar. "Do come on."

"Stay where you are," said the Ogre. "All of you. We can't possibly tackle that number." To their exasperation, he put his box down on the car bonnet and calmly sorted through the things in it. He took out a tin of sardines.

"But what about Johnny and Douglas?" Gwinny said, dancing with anxiety.

"What are you *doing*?" said Caspar.

"Hoping the old trick still works," said the Ogre, and threw the sardines with enormous force at a crash helmet bobbing in the middle of the scuffle.

The helmet immediately turned. They saw its owner go for the man nearest to him, evidently thinking he was the one who hit him.

"Oh, I see!" said Malcolm, and lifted a tin of peaches out of his own box.

"Not those," said the Ogre. "I like them. Sardines and baked beans only."

He shared them out. Caspar weighed a tin of beans in his hand, liked the weight, and hurled it into the crowd. He and Malcolm both scored direct hits on crash helmets, and the Ogre scored another. Each man they hit immediately turned on his neighbor. Within seconds, the whole group was savagely fighting among itself. Black-leather arms and legs whirled. There were fierce shouts in a strange language. Gwinny added to the confusion by missing with her baked beans and producing an enormous clang, which must have been the dustbin.

The Ogre threw Caspar the car keys. "Unlock it and get yourselves and this stuff in," he said. "Leave a door open for us." He set off at a run for the milling motorcyclists and fought his way in among them. He disappeared completely almost at once. Gwinny wrung her hands in despair and could think of nothing else. Malcolm had to push her into the car.

They were hurriedly loading in the boxes, when the Ogre reappeared backwards from the fight, dragging Johnny and Douglas. Johnny and Douglas were pale and disordered, but they still had the mop, the broom, and both parts of the dust-bin. Gwinny's tin was rolling thunderously about in the dustbin with the strawberry soap. They came panting up to the car and the Ogre thrust them into it. Nobody was sure how they all got in, but somehow they did it, and the Ogre fell into the driving-seat and started the engine. By this time, the motorcyclists were rolling in a heap on the ground, punching, kicking, and even biting one another.

"Aren't we going to do anything about them?" Caspar asked.

"No," said the Ogre breathlessly. "We can leave that to the police."

"But what happens when they turn out not to have names and addresses and things?" Malcolm wanted to know.

"I haven't the faintest idea," said the Ogre, backing briskly down the lane away from the struggle. "The police can think of something. Douglas, can you possibly lower that dustbin so that I could see something else in the mirror?"

Douglas tried, and produced yells of pain from Gwinny and Caspar. "I'm afraid I can't."

"Then I'll have to guess," said the Ogre. He turned round at the end of the lane, missing another car by what Malcolm said was less than half an inch, and sped across the gravel to the exit, with the dustbin jouncing deafeningly. "Douglas," he said loudly, "this was entirely due to your high-handedness. If you do anything like that again, I'll leave you to your fate." Douglas answered with a shamed mutter. "And," said the

Ogre, "please let this be the last chemical event. If there are any more, I think I may go mad."

They assured him that it would be, and they meant it. But they were reckoning without Gwinny. As they were carrying the boxes in through the back door, she gave a cry and threw herself on her hands and knees by the doorstep. Caspar, who nearly fell over her, wanted to know, rather loudly and angrily, what she thought she was doing.

"My pretty hairgrip!" said Gwinny. "Please help me find it. It's so pretty."

"Humor her," said Johnny. "She was born like that."

So they all put down their boxes again and, with some exasperation, hunted for the hairgrip. As Douglas said, it was like looking for a needle in a haystack.

Five minutes later, the Ogre said, "Is this it?" He stood up holding something bright and yellowish.

"Oh yes!" Gwinny said, reaching for it eagerly.

But the Ogre lifted it out of her reach and turned round into the sunlight to see it properly. "Where did you get this, Gwinny? It's solid gold!"

"No, it's not," said Gwinny. "It can't be. It was just an ordinary one. I made it pretty like that with Peter Fillus."

"What or who is Peter Fillus?" said the Ogre, still holding the hairgrip out of reach.

"It's just some little stones out of Malcolm's chemistry set," said Gwinny. "They're called Peter Fillus, and if you rub them on things they go pretty. I did my people some candlesticks. But they don't work on carpets and tables and things."

"Just metal?" asked the Ogre, with a strange expression on his face.

"That's right," said Gwinny.

"Fetch Peter Fillus here and let me see it," said the Ogre, handing back the hairgrip.

While the others brought in the boxes, the dustbin, the mop, and the broom, Gwinny sped upstairs and clattered down again breathless, holding a test-tube half full of small stones.

"That's all there is now," she explained.

"I expect it will do," said the Ogre and, still with the strange expression on his face, he carefully took out one small chip of stone and rubbed it along the handle of the dustbin lid. The place where the stone had touched immediately became a long golden streak.

"That's real gold?" said Douglas.

"I think it may be," said the Ogre. "My guess is that Peter Fillus is the Philosopher's Stone—and that's supposed to turn base metal into gold."

"Then we're rich," said Johnny. "Shall I get some money?"

The Ogre laughed. "No. Money won't do, because we'd never get away with it. But any other metal thing that we don't want—things that people might think were valuable—"

"Really horrible things, you mean?" asked Caspar.

"The more horrible the better," said the Ogre.

There was a rush for metal, which rapidly became a competition to find the ugliest thing in the house. Gwinny proudly brought out a bloated silver teapot. Caspar fetched a set of spoons with handles like ships in full sail that were designed to hurt your hand, no matter how you held them. Malcolm produced a huge, twiddly toast-rack someone had given the Ogre and Sally for a wedding present; and Johnny capped that with some fire irons on a stand disguised as three dolphins. They found a brass corkscrew with a simpering swan for a handle, a tormented iron cage for putting plants in, and a copper vase shaped like a rabbit. The Ogre found an ashtray that everyone agreed looked like a man-eating fungus, and a gilded model of a horse frantically trying to get loose from a clock grafted onto its hind legs. But it was Douglas who produced the cream of the collection. After a long and patient search, he came into the kitchen carrying a pair of stainless steel candlesticks shaped like hen's legs. Each had a clawed foot, and under that a ball on a pedestal. Above the claw was a long scaly leg, and, above that, metal feathers. The feathers just stopped at the top, and there was a hole for the candle there.

"Eughk!" said Gwinny, and the others looked at them with deep respect.

"First prize to Douglas," said the Ogre. "But there isn't much of this Peter Fillus. A careful selection, please. Those spoons are nickel silver, so they're out for a start. And I know that teapot has a silvermark, more's the pity. Those fire irons—Yes, I know, Johnny, but whoever heard of a golden poker? We'll have to choose things a jeweller would want to give us money for. Let's take the hen's legs, the horrified horse, that toast-rack, the copper bunny, and— What's this?" He picked out of the heap a hollow aluminum cow with a hole in its back.

"It's a jug," explained Caspar, who knew it well. "You hold it by its tail, and it sort of vomits milk through its mouth."

"Ah!" said the Ogre, profoundly pleased. "This, too, then."

"I say," said Douglas, surveying the selected horrors, "is

there any chance these would make enough money to buy us a bigger house?"

"That was my idea," admitted the Ogre.

This was enough to inspire everyone. They took the chosen horrors through to the dining room, with pork pies to sustain them, and set to work with the tiny chips of stone. Caspar and Douglas took a hen's leg apiece. Gwinny worked on the copper rabbit and Johnny on the hollow cow. These were all quite simple things, soon finished and gleaming. So Johnny and Gwinny went to lean over the Ogre and point out to him the parts of the agonized horse he had missed. Malcolm rubbed diligently away at his toast-rack. After a while, Caspar and Douglas tore themselves away from admiring their candlesticks and helped Malcolm. By this time, the stones were worn away to slivers and powder. They collected the grains on the end of their fingers—rather inconvenienced by the Ogre's pipe, which was wandering hopefully in between, hunting up crumbs of pork pie—and Malcolm used an accidentally gold-tipped knitting-needle to work Peter Fillus into the twiddles of the toast-rack.

The Ogre finished the horse. There were still a few grains of Peter Fillus left, so, as a joke, he fetched the fateful bucket and gave it a golden rim. "A reminder of the bad old days," he was saying, when Sally came in from the kitchen.

She was looking ten years younger for her short holiday. When she saw the bucket, the pipe, and the table laden with golden horrors, she stopped short in amazement. "Good heavens!" she said. "What *are* you doing?"

They rushed at her, clamoring explanations and welcome. She laughed. Half an hour later, when everything was explained, she was still laughing, but she seemed a little discontented, too. "Well, I feel a bit left out," she said, when the Ogre asked her what was the matter. "And I wish you'd waited with the Peter Fillus. I've got something worse than any of those."

"What?" said the Ogre.

"Aunt Violet's bequest," said Sally. "I'll show you."

She went to the cupboard and brought out from the very back something that was like quantities of metal ice cream cones on springs, with an extra large cone in the middle. It was very big and very ugly, and they had not the least idea what it could be.

"It's called an epergne," said Sally. "Now don't you wish you'd waited for me?"

They had to admit that it beat even the hen's legs.

Much later, when it was growing dark, Gwinny remembered her people, left out in the garden in their dollhouse. She hurried out to bring them in. To her dismay, the dollhouse was empty. Her people had gone. They had taken their golden candlesticks and their wax fruit, and a number of other things besides, and it looked as if they did not mean to come back. Nevertheless, Gwinny hopefully left the dollhouse in the garden for a week. But her people never came back. It seemed they must have set off in search of somewhere better to live. Gwinny was very hurt.

"They might at least have left me a note!" she said.

"You wouldn't have been able to read their language," Malcolm pointed out.

"It doesn't matter. It would have been polite," Gwinny said. But the fact was, her people had never been at all polite. In a way, she was relieved that they had gone.

The Ogre took the golden horrors to be valued the next Monday. After some delay, they were all sent to London to be auctioned, where they fetched prices that staggered the children. The hen's legs and the anguished clock proved to be worth more than they had thought, even in their wildest dreams. They were considered curiosities. But it was the hollow cow that fetched the most. It was bought by a collector, who called it a Cow Creamer, and who paid through the nose for it—much, as the Ogre said, as the cow poured milk—a price that amazed even the Ogre.

"Just think how much he might have paid for Aunt Violet's epergne," Sally said wistfully. "I wish you'd *waited.*"

They were able to move into a larger house almost at once, where, they all admitted, they were much happier. Everyone had a room to himself. Caspar and Douglas could play Indigo Rubber to their hearts' content. The Ogre was still often forced to bellow for silence, but, now everyone knew that his bark was so much worse than his bite, nobody let his roars trouble them. And the Ogre said he was growing hardened to living in a bear-garden.

Malcolm took his pencils with him to the new house. For some months, they hopped round his room at night. But, like the stick-insects they rather resembled, they did not live very long. Soon, only the Ogre's pipe was left to remind them of the chemistry sets. And as time went on, even that began to seem less like an animal and more like a pipe again. It spent longer and longer propped stiffly in the pipe-rack, and seldom purred when the Ogre smoked it. They thought the *Animal Spirits* must be gradually wearing off it.

After his pencils died, Malcolm began to suggest going back

to the old man's shop to see what else he had to sell. So, in the end, Caspar went there with him. He was very much afraid they would get sold something worse than pink footballs or the chemistry sets. But the shop was gone. Where the dark court had been, they found a wide hole full of mechanical excavators. Next time they saw it, the space was filled with an office-block even taller than the Ogre's. That seemed to be the last of Magicraft.